MAYHEM
A Detective Matt Deal Thriller

Stephen Bentley

Hendry Publishing

BACOLOD CITY, PHILIPPINES

Stephen Bentley/Hendry Publishing
www.hendrypublishing.com
Contact: info@hendrypublishing.com

Cover Art by www.thebookkhaleesi.com
Edited by S. Lee
Mayhem/Stephen Bentley. -- 1st ed.
Print ISBN 978-621-96190-9-7

A huge thank you to all the wonderful team behind my writing. That includes all my beta readers and VIP Readers Group.

Thank you too, Sheryl, for another wonderful editing job.

Thanks also to Zabrina, my wife, for her continuing unswerving support.

- Stephen Bentley

"Power does not corrupt. Fear corrupts... perhaps the fear of a loss of power."

— John Steinbeck

A NOTE FROM THE AUTHOR

Before you start reading *Mayhem*, Book Two in the Detective Matt Deal Thriller series, please permit me to mention the timeline. I believe it may help some readers.

This book starts in the year 2031 following the events that took place in *Mercy*, Book One in the series. That book starts in the year 2024 with the dreadful assault on Deal's daughter, Mercy.

Though set in the future, neither of the books in the series are dystopian novels. There are elements of dystopia but only to permit me as the author to fictionalise events to fit the storyline.

I also believe Book Two can be read as a standalone but as with almost all series, it may make more sense if you, the reader, tackle the books in order.

CONTENTS

CHAPTER ONE

WORDS

November 2031 - Tallahassee Memorial Hospital, Florida

Pain, heartache, and anxiety are words that somehow don't feel adequate when the person you love is undergoing emergency surgery for a gunshot wound. I not only love Anna; she is my soulmate. What I felt inside is almost beyond words. I can only say I felt hollow as if some being had sucked all the vitality out of me. Waiting for news is unbearable, but I felt grateful for some company.

I looked at my old friend Elaine Steele and asked, "How long has she been in surgery?"

As thankful as I was for Special Agent Elaine Steele's comforting presence, I struggled to shift the image of Anna wheeled through to the OR for surgery. How helpless she looked. She seemed limp, lifeless. *Not again*, I thought, *please God, not Anna too.*

I was thinking of my daughter, Mercy, who was not dead - but I would never see her alive again. Well, not *alive* in the full sense of the word as she lay in a continuing coma a few miles away in another hospital as a consequence of the brutal attack on Destin Beach. It stopped her life in its tracks and changed my life forever—a coma that had lasted seven years. I then thought of the events of the past few hours. We had arrived by helicopter at Tallahassee Memorial Hospital, then Anna was rushed into the OR. The same fragments of conversation kept running through my mind, just like a movie reel playing inside my head.

> *"Matt. Tell them to save the baby. You hear me? The baby... our baby."*

> *"Did you know Anna was pregnant?" Elaine's voice echoed, as did my reply.*

> *"No. I had no idea."*

I felt claustrophobic in the cramped, quiet room on the third floor of the Tallahassee Memorial Hospital. It was part of the space used to accommodate hospital security and visiting law enforcement officers. I had long since stopped picking at the doughnut, and my industrial coffee was now cold. It tasted crap when it was warm. Glancing at my watch for what was probably the fortieth time, I broke the silence between Steele and me. "How long has she been in surgery?" I repeated, or had I said that once only? I didn't know.

"Over three hours," Special Agent Elaine Steele said.

Back in my deep thoughts, I knew Anna was in expert hands. Anna, as she was known to Steele and me, but others knew her as Wolfie—a loner until she had met me soon after Mercy had been raped and left for dead. Many folks thought I was crazy leaving Wolfie Jules in charge of the gym. At the time, I'd gone to England, becoming a detective in the new National Crime Agency, but I knew she was 'the one' and trusted my instincts. My mind raced back in time to the night I first met her.

I recalled every detail. I had looked Wolfie up and down, taking in her five-foot-nothing stature, slim build, her leather biker jacket, and the fierce expression in her eyes, partly shielded by a wild fringe of black hair. She looked thirtyish, maybe mid-thirties. She was olive-skinned, kind of Spanish or Mexican looking. It turned out she was partly Cajun with a further hint of Louisiana in her family name of Jules, which I thought didn't sound French at all. I found her the most attractive woman I had seen in a long time. Stop! She was hot. Her most striking feature was a black eye patch over her right eye. I thought she looked like an extra out of *Pirates of the Caribbean.*

Steele probably saw I was deep in thought so repeated, "Matt, I said over three hours."

"What? Sorry, I was thinking."

"You asked me how long she has been in surgery."

"Yeah, I did. Is it that long?" I said. I was unable to concentrate, and without thinking I elected for the simple way of coping with my anxiety. I did small talk with Steele, asking, "What about you?"

I guess it nonplussed her, as she queried, "How do you mean?"

"Guys? Boyfriends? Lovers? You know," I said.

"Matt, I have only just got my feet down on Florida *terra firma,* and you ask me about guys," she snapped and then halted, and her face told me she wished she could cut off her tongue. "Sorry, it's hospitals. They have that effect on me." I knew this was a lie, but she continued, "Yes, I have met a guy. Early days though."

"Give. I want to know more," I said because this was taking my mind off Anna for a few moments.

"Well, not much to tell really. He's an officer in the Mexican Army, Miguel Diaz, but he prefers Mike. Good looking, gracious manners and smart."

"How the heck did you meet him?"

"At Quantico. He was giving a lecture on drug cartels and we met over coffee. You don't need to know the rest," Elaine said.

All conversation stopped on seeing a doctor enter the room, still in scrubs. I held my breath, dreading what news we were about to receive. As soon as he introduced himself as the surgeon who had operated on Anna and broke the latest update to us, Elaine Steele and I ran all the way to find her. To hell with walk, don't run.

Colonel Miguel Diaz was a Tejano, born in Nuevo Laredo in Mexico but raised in Crystal City, Texas. At the same time Matt and Elaine Steele were talking about him, he was paying his respects to the memory of his parents, an annual event when Diaz took leave from his military duties and visited the graveyard in Crystal City, Texas, where they lay buried.

A tall, almost six feet two inches, powerfully built man he laid the flowers on his parents' graves and said a silent prayer. After making the sign of the cross, he retired to a nearby bench to rest up a while before he drove back over the border to Mexico. From the seat, he watched a gaily coloured butterfly alight on a flowering bush. It made him think of the chaos theory as he watched its wings flip up, then down in a rhythmic beat. Diaz did this every year since his parents died, and the same memories came flooding back to him. Memories of a fifteen-year-old boy etched into the mental archive that made him the man he was today.

In his mind's eye, he could still see the group in his parents' modest home in Crystal City. Everyone was in the kitchen. "Don't kill them," a fifteen-year-old Miguel Diaz screamed at the Mexican.

Laughing, the man known as El Loco said, "*Cabrón*, stupid child. They refuse my orders. How else do I make sure people do as I tell them?"

"*Madre, Padre*, please tell him you will do it," Miguel pleaded.

"We will not take his dirty drug money back to Mexico. We came to Texas to get away from all that," Miguel's father said.

"You kill them, you kill me. If you don't, I will kill you one day, I promise you," Miguel shouted.

El Loco snorted another line of cocaine before speaking to Emilio, a sicario–a hired killer. Emilio was one of his men who had gone with him on the Texas trip purely to enforce El Loco's 'laws.' "*Mátalos,* Emilio, kill them."

Four shots rang out—two for each parent. Miguel's mother and father lay dead on the kitchen floor, shot in cold blood in front of their loving son.

Before leaving, El Loco said, "*Pendejo,* you live and tell the tale. El Loco will kill anyone who refuses orders, *¿Entender?*"

Miguel Diaz reached for a carving knife set on the kitchen table. As he took hold of it, Juan, another of El Loco's sicarios, pistol-whipped the boy on the side of his head, knocking him unconscious.

Just as if he were regaining consciousness, Diaz pulled out from his memories and muttered under his breath, "One day, one day. My time will come." Colonel Miguel Diaz walked back to his car. Starting the engine, he drove back to Mexico to carry out his regular duties as the officer in charge of an incorruptible but small elite army task force.

CHAPTER TWO

THE CORTEGE

Ten Days Later – Circle-K Store, Tallahassee, Florida

Sara Jo Montgomery was still in shock; not quite believing the news of two of her regular customers slain in such a callous manner. She knew State Troopers Chuck Roper and Arnie Regan well, almost like family to her. Chuck's second wife was expecting their first baby and Arnie's one and only wife was pregnant for the second time. As manager of the Circle-K store just short of I-10 close to the Tallahassee Automobile Museum, she would often serve coffee and a sandwich to the two men. She delighted in catching up on their latest news. That was what happened the day two Mafia hitmen shot them dead in cold blood. As she thought about the widows and kids who would never know their fathers, the tears flowed, and she made an instant decision. "To hell with it," she called out, "I'm going out there to watch the cortege. Margaret, watch the store for a while."

Margaret Hennessey, the new assistant, called back, "I got it. Now, pay your respects."

The cortege was all of a quarter mile long with two black hearses leading the way, flanked by Florida Highway Patrol motorcycle outriders. The motorcycle cops were from Troop H, the same troop the slain cops had belonged to. The hearses each contained an occupied coffin identically decorated with floral arrangements of which the two largest spelt out messages:

'Service, Courtesy, Protection'—the Florida Highway Patrol motto and a simpler 'We Love You, Daddy' from the widows and the unborn children of two of Florida's Finest.

Sara Jo cried on reading the last poignant message. She stayed rooted to her vantage point next to the highway. She didn't move until she watched the last of the following black and tan coloured police cars marked with the FHP logo and 'State Trooper' decals disappear as they proceeded slowly on the way to their destination. The Tallahassee Gardens Cemetery was to be the last resting place of two brave men. The patrol cars were from all over the state, with local police drafted in to patrol the highways in their temporary absence.

She was turning to walk back the few yards to the Circle-K when a man's voice jolted her from her thoughts. "Terrible day," he said. "I knew the two R's well. It could have been me." Turning again to locate the voice, she saw a man dressed casually in jeans and a tan windcheater. He smiled.

"How did you know them?" Sara Jo asked.

"I'm a state trooper too," he said fingering an FHP button pinned to his windcheater. "I was a relief trooper, so I teamed up with one or the other when one of them was on leave or called in sick."

"Funny, I never saw you with them. They often stopped for a coffee at the Circle-K," Sara Jo remarked.

"Before your time. The Circle-K and this strip-mall weren't here last time I teamed up with one of them. How's about I try your coffee?"

"Come, follow me and the coffee's on me. Can I ask you something?" Sara Jo said as she had suddenly thought of it and without waiting for an answer continued, "How is it you're not with the funeral cortege?"

"On my way to the oncologist at Tallahassee Memorial," he said. Sara Jo felt embarrassed, but the man put her at ease by adding, "Yeah, the Big C. I have a chemo appointment. That's why I'm not at the funeral. Besides, I'm not too keen on cemeteries just yet." He laughed as he spoke.

"Sorry to hear that. Come and have that coffee if you have time," she said.

Once inside, Sara Jo asked Margaret to bring a fresh jug of coffee while she talked to the man. "I'm Sara Jo, what's your name?"

"Brian, Brian Ryder. State Trooper Ryder, here's my badge," he said producing his identification.

"Good to meet you, Brian. Tell me as I'm such a nosy crone, are you still working?"

"So far, yes, but it might get to a point with the chemo where I'm too sick to even do what I'm assigned to right now."

"What's that? Some kind of light duties? I told you I was nosy," Sara Jo said smiling.

"Yeah, I look after the secure compound at the troop station location and garage in Mahan Drive, just off US90. I sit in the security booth all day, thinking positive thoughts," Ryder said with a chuckle.

"Way to go! You can beat it that way," Sara Jo said.

"I hope you're right," Ryder said, then finished his coffee before thanking Sara Jo and setting off for his chemo treatment.

CHAPTER THREE

VANITY

Two Days Later, Miami Beach, Florida

Lorey Hughes was now quite the socialite in Miami. Recently married to Professor Henry Braithwaite, an eminent brain trauma specialist, she, or rather he, could afford a luxury home on Miami Beach's Star Island. He preferred a condo near to the Research Department of the University of Miami, Neurosurgery Division, but she was younger than him and still sexy enough to… well, you know what I mean.

Hughes was her maiden name, and she also went by the same name in a professional capacity as an entertainments section editor for an international magazine. The professor need not feel slighted as she used Hughes when she was once married to Matt Deal. This is a woman who put the 'v' in vanity, so it was no surprise she hired a personal trainer as her first task on moving into 491, Star Drive, Star Island.

Once her trainer got to know Lorey, she wasn't the only one to believe the socialite also put the 'b' into bitch. The trainer thought Lorey was callous and for a good reason. Not once had Lorey Hughes either called or visited the Tallahassee hospital where her daughter, Mercy, lay lifeless in a coma. The trainer, Carla was her name, couldn't understand that on learning Lorey's ex had been responsible for killing two Mafia hitmen in the grounds of that same hospital. Still, she also learned Lorey never visited Mercy when her job meant she was based in London, England, not even when she took vacations back in Florida. Carla was also shocked to hear Lorey had responded to the news of the fatal shooting of her wealthy father, Jack Hughes, in his Pensacola home by saying, "Fuck him, I'm glad he's dead."

Carla had woken that Sunday morning with stomach pains. They probably saved her life. *I can't make the eleven-fifteen appointment with the bitch*, Carla thought. *Better call her. No, fuck her. I don't need her shit.*

It was 11:00 AM on Sunday, according to Lorey Hughes' Rolex, when she heard the doorbell chime. *It must be Carla*, she thought, *she's early*, as her appointment with her personal trainer was eleven fifteen. "I'm coming," she shouted down the hall, tying back her long blonde hair behind her head at the same time as admiring her leotard attired svelte body in the large hall mirror.

Lorey for once omitted to look through the side glass portion of the vast stainless-steel and glass double doors which were wide enough to accommodate a stampeding herd of elephants, and without a thought for security she opened the front door. Her jaw dropped when she saw a Hispanic man standing there, and for some weird reason, she knew they must hire a live-in helper to perform mundane tasks such as responding to callers. She didn't realise then such thoughts were too late.

In broken English, he said, "Lady, we are pool maintenance looking for new customers. Here is my card. Please take."

As Lorey Hughes took the business card, the man took hold of her roughly by the wrist. He turned her around, pushing her in the back, so she was now inside her own home. What she couldn't see were the man's accomplices following them inside. Before she could scream, a gun struck Lorey Hughes on the back of her head. She fell unconscious to the expensive marble tiles below her.

When she came to, she was bound to one of the dining room chairs that had been moved to the cavernous hallway. Her head hurt like hell, and through a fuzzy haze she saw her husband also bound to another dining room chair about three feet away. Then she looked down at her ankles. They had been roped together. Then a voice behind her. She thought it was the man at the door, the one who had forced her inside.

He said, "Lady, all we need to know is where we can find Matt Deal."

"How the hell would I know. He's my ex," she said defiantly.

She felt the gun strike her again with a blow to the right side of her head. Her ear rang and stars formed in front of her eyes for a moment.

"I ask you again. If you not tell me, I kill your husband," he said in less than perfect English.

Lorey Hughes sobbed, "I don't know. I'm telling you the truth." The voice behind her appeared to her right side. It was the same Hispanic she had spoken to at her front door. He didn't talk. Raising his pistol, he shot the professor twice through the middle of the forehead.

"Now, you know I am serious. Tell me now, or you will suffer."

CHAPTER FOUR

USE CAUTION

The Next Day - Star Island, Miami Beach, Florida

The black and white Miami Beach P.D. cruiser pulled silently into the driveway of the two-storey, nine-bedroomed luxury house behind the white Lexus SUV. Officers Ernesto Rodriguez, a twenty-year veteran, and rookie Paula Mercedes were responding to a call reporting Professor Henry Braithwaite, FRCS, a traumatic brain injury expert at the Research Department of the University of Miami, Neurosurgery Division, as missing. The caller, a secretary at the research department, also reported she could not contact either the professor or his wife, Lorey.

Rodriguez closed the driver's door quietly and by force of habit, unclipped the button on his gun holster, unsure of what to expect. Mercedes copied him and recalled the dispatcher using the ten-zero code—*use caution*. She was nervous as a kitten but bit her lip in steely determination to prove herself up to the task.

The cops padded up to the expansive glass and stainless-steel double doors at the front of the house just two yards beyond the Lexus, Rodriguez noting there was no one in the vehicle. He gestured to Mercedes to push open one of the double doors as it was slightly ajar, while he drew his pistol and adopted the firing position. Gun also pulled, Mercedes complied. The vast hall inside was empty except for two corpses.

The female was hanging upside down, tied at the ankles with rope and the rope secured to the bannister rail that ran along the landing on the upper floor. Her face, drained of all colour, hung about three feet off the hall floor. Pools of blood obscured the white marble floor tiles beneath her. Rodriguez, both appalled and fascinated, studied the corpse and saw the four incisions to her neck, two on each side.

"She's been left to bleed out," he said. "Call it in." Mercedes made for the front door. "Use your Rover. You don't need to go back to the cruiser."

Mercedes ignored her senior partner's advice to use her portable transceiver and, on rushing outside, vomited in some bushes alongside the drive. Disregarding his rookie partner, Rodriguez glanced over at the second corpse. It was a man bound to a chair with two crimson holes in his forehead. The body was facing the hanging corpse. A scream seemed to want to escape his lips, but no doubt stifled by the two slugs to his head.

"Sorry," Mercedes said after she returned to the crime scene, "I called it in from the cruiser."

"And?" Rodriguez said.

"Secure the scene and wait for the M.E. and forensics."

"Detectives?"

"Yes, them too."

"Okay, we wait then. You want to sweep the rooms up there?" Rodriguez asked, pointing upstairs. "Or check the backyard?"

"The yard," Mercedes said.

"Don't worry, the perps have long gone, but we are sticking to the protocol, right? And keep that weapon drawn, okay?"

Mercedes nodded as her mouth had dried up.

Forty-five minutes later, the M.E. was first to arrive. "This how you found them?" Mike Takisuma said.

"Not moved or touched a thing, Doc," Rodriguez said.

"Good. You know who they are?"

"No idea."

"He is, or was, I should say, a brilliant man in his field… brain trauma injury and stem cell research. English… married her… Lorey Hughes, socialite and bit-part entertainment editor. She was in the news lately."

"How come?" Rodriguez asked.

"Her daughter, Mercy, is in a coma in a Tallahassee hospital. Her ex, another Brit… Matt Deal… shot dead two wise guys in the hospital grounds."

"This connected, then?"

"No idea, but the detective division will investigate that. All I can say is this hanging upside down so the vic bleeds out slowly is a classic torture method used by the Mexican drug cartels."

"Friendly people," Mercedes said.

"Welcome to Miami," Mike Takisuma said.

Miguel Diaz got stuck into his first task of the day on returning to his elite task force unit in Nuevo Laredo. He sifted through the latest intelligence reports on Mexico's drug cartels, and one caught his attention. There was a confirmed report of the Hernandez twins, two of El Loco's most trusted hired killers – sicarios – having flown to Miami. Diaz knew they were specialists in torturing by hanging victims upside down before they cut the victim's neck and interrogating them before they bled out. That was one speciality – the other? Decapitating enemies of their *jefe*, El Loco, then hanging the heads suspended from bridges for the world to see.

Calling FBI Special Agent Elaine Steele on his cell phone, it delighted him to hear her voice. "Mike, I was wondering when you'd call. How are you?"

"Hey, Ellie, I'm good and you?"

"Okay, I guess, but I've been transferred like I thought I would," she said.

"Florida?"

"Yes. OCG, Organised Crime Group working out of Tallahassee."

"A tad closer to me," Diaz said, and Elaine Steele could sense the smile accompanying the words.

"Only the Gulf separates us," she said.

"As long as it's only a stretch of water, huh?"

"Yeah," Steele said.

"Ellie, a bit of intel. Two of El Loco's killers have flown into Miami. Thought you might want to know," Colonel Diaz said.

"Thanks, I'll pass it on to the Bureau in Miami. Speak soon, yes?"

"You got it. Take care, Ellie."

CHAPTER FIVE

WORSE THAN DEATH

Same Day - Mount Olivet Roman Catholic Cemetery, New Jersey

The turnout was just as expected for the funerals despite the snowstorm laying down another six inches on top of the icy streets. Mike Russo, the *capo* of the New Jersey mob, gazed at the two coffins lowered into the adjacent plots and whispered to his wife, "They must use a jackhammer to break up the earth." He was as irreverent in death as in life; after all, he was at the funerals of two of his best hitmen and loyal soldiers. To him, it was all part of the racket.

Carmen, his wife, elbowed his ribs. "Trust you. I guess they treat the earth as if it were concrete, breaking up frozen soil and adding fresh." She was right, not that her husband gave a damn.

Russo looked across to the black-clad widows of Andy Messina and Joe Caruso who gave him identical disapproving stares. He ignored them. *Don't you worry, Matt Deal is as good as dead.* That message was repeated later that day not only to the widows but also to his small army of wise guys. They were united in a desire to exact revenge on Deal and his lover, Wolfie Jules, for their part in killing Russo's best hitmen in Tallahassee, Florida.

Once the ceremonies were over, the cortege made its way to Russo's favourite Italian restaurant, *Bella Donna,* in nearby Linden. Brendan O'Rourke had also travelled from Atlanta to New Jersey for the funerals. He and Jack Hughes were long time business associates of Russo except Hughes was now dead. "Shame Jack can't be here," Russo said privately after the meal.

"Served him right. He should never have got involved with that Gonsales woman."

"Is that the construction foreman's wife? The one Andy and Joe capped?"

"The one and only. She shot herself after killing Jack. His widow was pissed coming home to find two dead bodies in her hall." Russo laughed. "Hear anything of Lorey Hughes, Deal's ex?" O'Rourke added.

"Taken care of. She knows nothing."

"Pity. I was hoping she may lead us to Deal."

"Right, I can assure you she knew nothing. What about that bitch of Deal? The one with the eyepatch," Russo said.

"I don't need reminding who she is. She and Deal murdered Conor."

"Okay, okay. I know all that. I know he was your son. Don't get all moody on me."

"Sorry. I just get mad thinking of them. She's still in the hospital in Tallahassee. Shame the slug didn't kill her outright, but last time I checked, she's on the critical list."

"The hospital, that's where we'll find him then. Brendan, worse things than death are about to come the way of Deal and his piece of pussy, I swear to you."

CHAPTER SIX

SNAKE BITE

Same Day - Florida

The temperature in Florida was nearly seventy degrees higher on the Fahrenheit scale than New Jersey. There was no need for jackhammers to prepare the burial plot for Randy. Pat Wilson wiped the tears away as his former buddy and special services colleague's casket was lowered. I placed an arm around his shoulder to comfort him when I noticed Pat give me the briefest quizzical look. Our eyes searched each other for less than a second. I did not react but made a mental note because it was something I didn't comprehend. It made me feel uneasy.

Neither of us mentioned it in my SUV on leaving the Destin Memorial Cemetery. There was an uneasy silence until Pat spoke. "A fucking snake, Matt. Can you believe that?"

"Rattler?" I said, concentrating on the road ahead.

"Yeah. Diamondback. That's why he didn't get off a kill shot when the two mob guys approached you and Wolfie."

"Kill shot? So, he did get one off?"

"Yeah. It's probably still travelling." Pat smiled. "I saw the recoil. It must have been a reflex when the rattler bit because the rifle was pointing up, not at his intended target."

"Good job we had you as back up on the grenade launcher, the RPG."

"Oh, yeah. Randy would have loved to see them smoked. You know, I got him to hospital, but it was too late. The venom had reached his heart. It stopped beating. All the scrapes we have been in, and a fucking snake sends him packing."

"Sorry, man. If it weren't for me, he'd still be here," I said.

"We did it for Wolfie. Well, for Sean really… and you. We know she thinks the world of you. And you're the best thing that could have happened to her after Sean died in Afghanistan."

"Thanks, and sorry for your loss. What say you we go visit Wolfie now?"

"In Tallahassee?"

"Sure, at the hospital."

"Okay," Pat said, laying his hand on my knee for a brief moment. "And thanks."

"For what?"

"The hand on the shoulder back at the graveside."

"Don't get any ideas," I said grinning. "Relax. Only kidding."

Traffic was light on the interstate, the I-10. I made it to the Tallahassee Memorial Hospital in just over two hours. Wolfie had been off ICU for ten days and was now recovering in a private room guarded by an agent assigned by Elaine Steele. She was now Special Agent in Charge of the FBI's Organised Crime Group Florida, based in Tallahassee following her sudden transfer from a Bureau assignment in D.C.

Peering into her room, I saw Wolfie had a visitor. Wolfie looked up and on seeing Pat and me, smiled radiantly. Her visitor turned to see what she was smiling about. "Matt, how are you?" Steele said.

"I'm good, Ellie." Turning to Wolfie, I added, "Anna, do you mind if I have a private one-on-one with Elaine for a few minutes? Pat can keep you company. Oh, sorry… Pat, this is Elaine Steele… Elaine, Pat."

Wolfie said, "Sure, but don't be long. I've got some good news from the doctor. Anyways, Pat can tell me how Randy's funeral went. Just too bad I couldn't have been there. Sean and Randy dead. So, be careful, Pat. You're the last of the three amigos."

"I won't be long, I promise," I said.

Leaving Pat and Wolfie to catch up, I found a quiet part of the third storey corridor to talk to Steele.

"How long is the security arrangement going to last, Ellie?" I said.

"A few days is all."

"After that?"

"She will be at home. The doctors have given Anna a clean bill of health. She will fully recover from the gunshot wound and deliver a perfectly healthy baby in about six months from now."

"Wow! I suppose Anna was about to tell me before I blundered in."

"Let it be a surprise, then. Let her think she is the first to tell you."

"I will."

"What's your plans, Matt?"

"About?"

"You are not stupid. I'm talking about your intentions about the remaining rapists and Brendan O' Rourke, the father. It was them who put Mercy where she is today, not more than ten miles from here, in a coma she'll likely never recover from. O'Rourke made sure none of those young bastards will ever be prosecuted when he bribed Captain Stevenson, the Fort Walton chief of detectives, to ensure the DNA evidence disappeared. Hell, why am I telling you all this? You know what happened but let me also say this. I think you and Anna got to the O'Rourke kid in Atlanta and it wouldn't surprise me if she got to Stevenson too, because you were in England at the time. I understand, Matt, but where's this leading?"

"You done?"

"Yes, so what do you have to say?"

"I'll tell you later. First, I need a favour."

"What?"

"Take me to the Highway Patrol HQ here in Tallahassee. I want to take a good look inside the stolen Ford pick-up truck Caruso and Messina were using. Your FBI badge can fix that."

"What do you expect to find?"

"I don't expect anything. I'm curious, and anyways it's best if you know nothing," I said, tapping my nose.

"Matt Deal, if I didn't know you better, I'd think you were up to no good."

"Moi?"

"Now I know it's no good when you do that French stuff," Steele said as she playfully punched my arm.

"Ha! That's what comes from working with me so long back in England. You know me too well. Come on, we'd better go talk to Anna."

CHAPTER SEVEN

GOOD NEWS

"So, what's the good news?" I said on re-entering Wolfie's room.

"The best. They say I'll make a complete recovery from the gunshot and even better, our baby is fine too," Wolfie said, looking radiant.

I stuck to the script, pretending it was all fresh news to me and I'd heard it first from Wolfie, so I said, "Wow! That is good news. It's fantastic!" I leaned over the bed and kissed Wolfie lightly on her cheek.

"Congratulations, you guys," Pat said and echoed by Elaine Steele.

"Anna, I need to go somewhere with Ellie. I promise it won't take long. Is that okay?" I asked.

"Sure, as long as it's not dangerous. I just want you back in one piece," Anna said. "Ellie, promise you'll take care of him."

"You got it. Pat, are you staying?" Steele said.

"Yes, we still got a bit of catching up," Pat said.

Pat stayed with Wolfie while Elaine drove me to the local Highway Patrol headquarters in Tallahassee.

One flash of her FBI shield got us into the secure compound where the cars were kept whether stolen and recovered, or the cops had other good reasons to keep them. The duty officer pointed us to the stolen car used by Messina and Caruso on the day of the fatal shootings of the two state troopers, Regan and Roper. Messina and Caruso had killed them before the two Mafia hit men were ambushed by me, Wolfie and her ex-husband's special forces chums, Randy and Pat. After pointing out the silver Ford truck, the duty officer added, "The owner wants to know when he can claim his truck."

"Soon," Steele said a bit huffily as she turned to walk over to the truck with me in tow, then realising she'd been sharp, glanced at the officer's name badge. "Very soon, Trooper Ryder."

"Okay, but let me know if you take anything for evidence. I need to log it. Are you the guy who capped the two wise guys?" Ryder said.

I said, "Yeah, with a little help."

"Good work. The world's a better place with those two rats dead. I knew both of those troopers. I teamed up with them as a relief driver sometimes and used to play poker with them. Hell, it could have been me," the cop said before watching us for a few moments, then returning to his position in the compound guard hut.

I started to search the truck but broke off when Steele said, "What are you looking for?"

"Tell the truth, I don't rightly know. It's just a hunch."

My search lasted three minutes. On opening the glove compartment, I found a cloth bag. Peeking inside, I soon realised what it held. "Chips. Casino chips," I said.

Holding one between her thumb and forefinger, Steele examined it. "Biloxi. The Grand Resort Casino and this one alone is worth one thousand dollars. These guys were high-rollers."

"You're right. There are maybe ten in there."

"What do we do?" Steele said.

"Leave them. They have tracking devices embedded in them, so the casino cage folks know exactly who they belong to. They're of no value to anyone else but these two dead wise guys."

Steele said, "Not much use to them now," as she pulled on the loose fascia on the inside of the front passenger door. Reaching inside to the bare metal, she pulled out a clear plastic bag. "These have value," she said indicating a bunch of smaller transparent sealed plastic bags inside the larger bag. "Looks like hundred-dollar bills."

I said, looking at the contents of the bags, "Yup, and a lot of them."

"What are we going to do with it?" Steele said.

"I know exactly what we do. Fancy a drive to Mobile? I need to see an old lady there. I'll tell you the story on the way. I'll call and let Anna know, and I can also drop by the gym to check in on Bobby."

"Okay, Matt. Hide the bag inside your jacket. Let's get outta here," Steele said. I knew she trusted me. I had worked with her for a long time.

"Can't miss it. Big Deal's Gym, trust you to come up with that name," Steele said as we pulled up outside the gym on Harbor Boulevard, Destin.

"Follow me, I'll introduce you to the staff."

On entering the street-level reception area, I said, "This is Sandy, Sandy Grant, our receptionist. Sandy, meet Elaine Steele, Special Agent Steele, I should say."

They exchanged brief pleasantries before I asked Sandy to ask Bobby Peters to buzz us in. While waiting for Bobby to do that, I said, "I hope he's keeping that locked all the time since the shooting. Is he, Sandy?"

"Yes, Matt. He's very security conscious since what happened in Tallahassee."

My murmur of approval was drowned out by the buzz of the electronic door locking system. "Upstairs, Ellie, follow me. See you later, Sandy."

Bobby Peters greeted us as we climbed the stairs, "Hey, Matt! Good to see you and your friend."

"Good to see you, too, and this is Special Agent Steele to you."

"Hi, Spec…"

"Knock that off. He's joshing you. Call me Elaine."

"She is a Special Agent though so watch your p's and q's, Bobby."

"Ignore him. He's only your boss."

"Come through to the office. Would you like coffee or tea or something?" Bobby said.

We declined the offer.

"You been doing as I told you? Keeping a sharp eye open for anything strange or anyone who remotely looks connected… like the Mob, or any freakin gangster for that matter," I said.

"I have, Matt, and not just here but when I get home too. I always make sure no one is following me."

"Good. Here's Wolfie's Glock. Make sure it's a bad guy if you shoot though, won't you?"

"Cool! You sure about this?"

"Matt discussed this with me, and I agreed it's a good idea. We don't know if the attempt on their lives was the only one or if it is to be the first of many, especially since Russo's best hitmen are both dead," Steele said.

"Listen up, Bobby. Elaine's the expert. She is the boss of the Bureau's Organised Crime Group here in Florida."

"Special Agent in Charge?" Bobby said.

"Yes, I am," she said.

"We can't stop long. Elaine and I need to see an old widow in Mobile. You remember her? You're the one who traced her."

"I do. A French name, I think."

"Correct. Celia Le Fevre. You did a great job finding her."

"Thanks, Matt."

"You're welcome, Bobby. Just make sure you continue looking out over your shoulder and never relax. We must keep security tight. What's Sandy doing these days? I mean, where is she living?" I said.

Bobby's face turned red, and he spluttered, "We live together, Matt, at my grandma's house."

"Good to hear. She's a nice young woman. Did you know she went to school with Mercy?"

"I did. She told me. You sure you don't want a coffee or something? I'm going downstairs to get a freshly brewed cup. I can bring some more back with me if you like," Bobby said in his pleasant eager to please manner.

Noting Ellie had shaken her head, I said, "No. We're good, thanks."

After Bobby left the office, I told Ellie how Wolfie had employed Bobby as manager when I was in the UK. I made Ellie laugh when I recounted the story of Bobby grabbing Anna by the ass while he was servicing Anna's cherished Harley. She laughed more when I threw in Anna's reaction: "Anna grabbed a wrench from the Harley seat and swung it, connecting with the side of Bobby's face. 'Never touch me again, boy. Do you hear?' she said."

Elaine said, "How did he react?"

"All he said was, 'Yes, ma'am.' I tell you, no one messes with Wolfie Jules. After that incident, he became a protector. Any time his friends made any comments about her, he told them straight to knock it off. Anna got word of that so employed him at the gym."

"That's good," Steele said. "And can I ask why Wolfie is Wolfie to all except you and me, Matt?"

"That's her choice. Goodness, that reminds me. Where's Sheba, Wolfie's dog?"

Bobby returned to the office with his coffee, so I asked him.

"My grandma is taking care of her," Bobby said. "How come you two know each other so well?"

Elaine said, "We were both detectives in London, England, first on the Human Trafficking Squad, then the newly formed National Crime Agency. I got sick of him, and that's when I got my secondment to the FBI in D.C." I said nothing, just smiled. "Let's go, Matt. Nice to meet you, Bobby."

CHAPTER EIGHT

MAYHEM WILL FOLLOW

During the drive from Destin through Pensacola and across the state line into Alabama, I was curious about Steele's plans. "You ever think of going back to London?"

"Yes, and I don't think I will go back."

"Think or know, Ellie?"

"Well, would you? The country's gone to the dogs since the Brexit fiasco. I have no idea what good people thought would come out of leaving the European bloc. Even though the Americans have propped up the economy, it's still a nightmare with no elections in sight for the foreseeable future. It's even worse than when you left and my god, it was bad then."

"I guess."

"Not a guess, Matt, don't you ever watch the BBC World News? Every night there's another inner-city riot."

"Race riots?"

"Race and mass unemployment."

"So, you'll stay with the Bureau?"

"Yes, as long as I don't screw up again."

"You mean the La Motta thing, the undercover cop who infiltrated Russo's mob?"

"Don't remind me, but yeah."

"Ellie, we're old friends so please don't take offence and I'm not prying. Is there anyone in your life these days? You strike me as rather lonely."

"Have you forgotten? I told you about the Mexican army officer."

"Yeah, sorry, but that was back at the hospital waiting for news about Anna. I was a tad distracted, you know?"

"I understand, and anyway his name is Mike in case you can't remember, but I don't want to say anything more just yet. You know, in case I'm wrong about the guy." I nodded, knowing Elaine had no wish to elaborate, and after a brief silence, Steele said, "And you? Not your love life, I can see you and Anna are great together. Your plans about what you're going to do about Russo and O'Rourke. I asked you at the hospital, and you said, 'I'll tell you later,' so tell."

"If you really must know, I plan to kill all of them for what they did to Mercy. I will also kill anyone who comes after me seeking revenge over the killings of Caruso and Messina. It's as simple as that."

"This simple, huh? Don't mess with Deal or mayhem will follow."

"You got it."

"Let me tell you something, Matt Deal. I hope you change because though understandable, all that vengeance stuff will eventually be your downfall and it will eat you up inside."

"I heard you. Now swing off at the next ramp. We are going to see an old lady who deserves some good news."

Elaine Steele's mind wandered back to a recent time at Quantico, the FBI's Training Academy, located in Virginia. She was having coffee in the cafeteria, waiting to give a talk on her specialist subject of handling and running undercover agents when a big guy wearing a black leather jacket paired with smartly pressed grey slacks asked if he could join her. He introduced himself as Colonel Miguel Diaz of the Mexican Army but spoke with an attractively rich Texas accent. After taking in his rugged good looks, she nonchalantly waved her arm, rather pleased he had singled her out.

As an ice breaker, Elaine Steele asked Colonel Miguel Diaz, "How is it they sent an army officer on this Quantico course?"

The tall Mexican laughed. "I'm here to educate the FBI. I'm not a student."

Blushing, which Diaz found attractive and amusing in equal measure, Steele said, "Oh, how stupid of me."

"Not at all," he said with a masculine grace which immediately set Steele's pulse racing because she sensed here was a rare being – a man with sensitivity – at least rare in her line of work where men seemed to beat their chests and go in for dick-waving competitions. Mind you, there was an exception, and that was Detective Matt Deal, but it was a long time since she had worked with Matt back in her detective days in London. And anyway, she reminded herself, Matt had a new woman in his life.

"I'm here to talk about Mexican drug cartels and in particular the Los Zetas cartel," he added.

"Ah, yes. El Loco's mob. Tell me, that surely can't be the same El Loco who ran that cartel in the 2020s?"

"No, it's his son, but he's worse than his father ever was."

"You make it sound like you know him," Steele said.

"Yes, I do, and if you let me take you to dinner tonight, I'll tell you all about it."

Blushing once more, Steele said, "I'd like that."

"Right. Eight tonight, meet you at the gate. I'll drive. You can tell me all about London. I've never been there."

Elaine Steele heard Matt say sharply, "Ellie." She thought she had been driving on autopilot as she shelved her memories and concentrated on Deal's directions, taking them to the trailer home of Celia LeFevre.

CHAPTER NINE

FBI LADY

I thought Elaine was distracted because she seemed startled when I gave her the last of the directions to Mrs Le Fevre's home. As we drove into the trailer park, I saw her trailer. It looked even more ramshackle than my last visit. This time, I didn't show my Florida P.I. identification after knocking on the door, but instead had Steele show her FBI badge. After a few moments, I heard the familiar southern drawl making a weak, throaty inquiry, "Who is it?"

"Detective Deal, Matt Deal, Mrs LeFevre. You remember me, I hope."

"I remember y'all. I'm in a wheelchair, not stupid. You gotta another woman in tow. Where's that last one. Pretty thing. Eye patch. Unusual name… Wolfie or sumtin?"

"That's why I've come to see you."

The door opened an inch. Celia LeFevre appeared in her rickety old wheelchair. "You better come in then. FBI lady now. What happened to your girlfriend, the one with the patch? She not dead, is she?"

I reassured the old lady first before taking a seat at the improvised dining table. "No, she's not dead, but she did get shot."

"My dear Lord! Is she okay?"

"She is, Mrs LeFevre…"

"Please, Celia."

"She is recovering in a Tallahassee hospital. She should be home sometime soon."

"That is good news. And who is this young woman?"

"I'm Elaine Steele, ma'am."

"You English too?"

"Yes, ma'am. Matt and I were detectives together in London some years back."

"Good. I like the English. Good manners."

That's what she said last time, I thought.

"Tell me, why did such a pretty girl get shot?"

"The same two gangsters who killed your husband, Peter, they did it trying to kill me," I said.

"I hope they're dead. Did you kill them?"

"Finished them off after some friends blew up their vehicle."

"Now, wait a minute. I saw that on the news channel. Tallahassee?"

"Yes," I said.

"And I recognise you now, FBI lady, I saw you standing by a helicopter. Am I right?"

"Yes," Steele said.

"They killed two Highway Patrol troopers too if I remember correctly."

"Sadly, that's also true, ma'am," Steele said.

"What can I do for you, then?"

"It's more what I can do for you, Celia," I said as I placed the envelope on the tabletop. "I counted it. There's exactly sixty-thousand dollars. Let's say the gangsters are returning what they stole from you and your husband."

"I didn't say they stole sixty. I said about fifty or sixty thousand."

"Some interest." I smiled.

"Suppose you want a receipt?"

"No. We were never here, okay?" I said.

Celia LeFevre, aged about fifty-three going on seventy-three, broke down and cried. Sobbing, she murmured, "God Bless you, son. God Bless you."

"Ma'am, we will make sure you are feeling okay before we let ourselves out," Steele said.

"That's kind of you both. I am fine. Tell me this, Detective Deal, do you still seek retribution for what happened to your daughter?"

"How do you know about Mercy?"

"I gone and told y'all. I saw it all on the local news channel. It made the Panhandle news because of what happened to your daughter in Destin, terrible thing."

"The short answer is, Celia, I do and won't rest until they are all dead and buried."

"Mister, you are a good man, and I'm gonna tell you this because it's the god's truth. That revenge and hate in your heart will cause you more pain unless you get rid of it all. Do that for me, please, son."

"Sorry I cannot."

"I told him the same on the way here," Steele said.

"Well, it's up to him, missy, I'd say… but perhaps he's a stubborn mule," were LeFevre's parting words.

CHAPTER TEN

WISE WOMAN

Steele dropped me off at the Tallahassee Memorial Hospital before she went to her upscale temporary rented apartment home in Old Bainbridge Road, Tallahassee. Before driving off, she reminded me once more, "She's a wise woman. Listen to her. At the very least, talk to Anna about it." I felt like asking, 'Who?' but I knew she was talking about Celia, so instead I ignored my old friend. *Stubborn mule*, I knew she thought because I saw it writ large on her face. That's what happens after you have worked so long with people. Things can be said or unsaid, and the unsaid can still have meaning.

Settled in for the night, Steele's mind drifted back to Mike Diaz and she couldn't rid herself of a feeling of desolate loneliness after she recalled every last detail of their first date.

They met for dinner as arranged. Diaz drove them north on I-95 to Dale City in his Avis rental, finding a nice restaurant to spend the next few hours getting to know one another better. Little did she know, they were about to share things they usually kept bottled up inside. The one thing she never confessed to was her feeling of loneliness, but he wasn't stupid, far from it, and Mike Diaz knew she was.

First, he asked all about her time in London and the reasons for her secondment to the FBI, then he understandably quizzed her about Matt Deal. Elaine Steele started with Matt. "He was my detective partner on the Human Trafficking Squad in London, then later on the newly-formed National Crime Agency."

"Is it true that's modelled on the L.A.P.D.?" Diaz asked.

"Yes, right down to the handbook and choice of weapons. There's even a robbery-homicide squad which Matt and I worked together."

"Elaine, I must ask you this, were you and Matt lovers?"

"Call me Ellie, please. Yes and no is my truthful answer." She paused, wondering how much to say, but soon relaxed as she felt secure with this man. "We jumped into bed a few times, and it's true to say we were and still are fond of each other, but commitment was not on the agenda for either of us. Matt was still grieving over the loss of Mercy."

"Mercy?" Diaz said.

"Matt's daughter."

"She died?"

"As good as. She was fifteen when she was gang-raped, beaten and left for dead on a Destin beach. She's been in a coma ever since."

"My God!" Diaz exclaimed.

"Precisely, and it was after that, Matt decided to go to England. He is British, you see, but a naturalised US citizen too."

"Why flee?"

"He was threatened by Jack Hughes, his then father-in-law, a nasty piece of work who was Mob connected. He figured he didn't have much choice, but every year he took a whole month's vacation to visit Mercy in the hospital, which is more than his ex-wife ever did."

"A good cop?"

"The best. He looked after me in some sticky situations. A lot of cops didn't like him, they thought he was aloof, but I think that was his way of trying to deal with the loss of his daughter. He didn't suffer fools. It was the NCA's loss when he came back to Florida."

"He's back? Do you see much of each other?"

"Came back after he was prosecuted for killing a perp who was trying to kill him. And no, we don't see each other. He's got a fine woman now who's like a sister to me."

"What's he doing then?"

"Came back to his Destin gym business and opened a P.I. business."

"Sorry to pry, so, what about you?"

"Me? I'm just dandy apart from…" Steele hesitated.

"From what?"

"I shouldn't be telling you this, but I'm worried."

"I'm listening if you care to confide in me." Diaz smiled, and his eyes spoke warmth and compassion to Steele.

"I think I may be fired." Steele sighed.

"Why?"

"Listen, this is all hush-hush stuff, okay?"

"My lips are sealed," Diaz said, and Elaine looked at his mouth and wanted to kiss his lips. She smiled at the thought.

"I was the main handler of a UC. He got killed."

"An undercover agent?"

"Yes."

"Was it your fault he got killed?"

"No, but the bureau has to have a scapegoat… and it seems that's me."

"Fuck them," Diaz said.

"Yeah, fuck them," Steele agreed as they both laughed. "What's your story, Mike, now you have unlocked my secrets?"

"Me? I'm a Tejano, born in Nuevo Laredo in Mexico but raised in Texas, so I have dual nationality. I moved back to Mexico after my mom and pop died."

"Then you joined the Mexican Army?" Elaine asked.

"I did."

"Why?"

"The Federales, *Policía Federal,* and the provincial police are corrupt and many in the Army too, but I figured it was the least corrupt outfit I could join in fighting the drug cartels."

"This has something to do with the deaths of your parents, right?"

"Yes, you mentioned El Loco earlier today. It was El Loco and his men who murdered my parents in cold blood."

"Why? What happened?" Steele said.

"The short version is they killed them because they refused to smuggle cash over the border into Mexico."

"Cash?"

"United States dollars, the proceeds of El Loco's people selling drugs in Texas."

"I'm sorry," Steele said.

"Thank you. It's part of the price we all pay for the crazy war on drugs as you gringos call it."

"Gringo? You sound and act more American than Mexican if you don't mind me saying so. So, Mike, what's the answer to the war on drugs?"

"No answer, or none that I have. All I know is it's a waste of time, money, and many lives."

"We can't just allow the cartels and organised crime gangs to do as they please though, can we?"

"No, that's why we both have jobs," Diaz said at which they both laughed loudly.

"Tell me honestly, Mike, do you believe in retribution?"

"In the case of El Loco, I do. And one day I hope to bring it on personally – *a mano a mano.*"

"Hmm," Steele uttered.

"You disapprove?"

"Not really approve or disapprove. I guess that is what goes through Matt's head. I don't think he will rest until he exacts revenge on all those connected to the rape of Mercy."

"You must be careful. Sit on the fence, and you are likely to get hurt, my friend. We are engaged in a dangerous business where there is no place for the fainthearted. Sad but true, I'm afraid to say."

"Mike, stay with me tonight," Steele said.

"How can I say no to a beautiful woman like you?"

"You can't."

CHAPTER ELEVEN

SECURITY

On arriving at the hospital after Steele had dropped me off, I walked past the FBI agent detailed to watch over Wolfie. He gave me a peremptory nod of the head before scanning the hospital corridor for unwanted visitors. On opening the door, I found Anna alone in her private room. By the looks of it, I thought she had just finished a meal, partly confirmed when she asked, "Have you had anything to eat?"

"I'm fine, Anna, how are you feeling?"

"Right as rain. I can't wait to get out of here, not that I'm ungrateful. They did a fine job of patching me up. Look how neat this scar is," she said, pulling up her gown to reveal a thin line of pink scar tissue on her groin.

"Looks kinda sexy," I said.

"Crazy Deal."

"I mean the pink against that sexy dusky skin."

"If you're getting horny, mister, you will have to wait until you get me home."

"You know you make me horny, but we need to talk about our security arrangements once the hospital discharges you."

"You think they will come after you again?"

"Me and you. I don't know for sure, but they are the Mob, and we did take out two of their guys."

"Are you saying we shouldn't go home?"

"I'm saying we might be safer in the bunker for a while."

"Our secret love nest," Anna laughed.

"And I've given your Glock to Bobby."

"Good, we have other weapons at the bunker anyways."

"He's got Sheba round at his grandma's house, and that's not all. Did you know he is dating Sandy?"

"Matt, how would I know, I've been in here since the shooting. I'm pleased his grandma is taking care of Sheba. As for Sandy, she's old enough to know what she's doing."

"Oh, I almost forgot, Ellie and I just got back from Mobile. We gave Celia LeFevre sixty grand we found in Caruso and Messina's car. If you recall, they stole cash from them after they shot and killed her husband."

"Bet she was delighted."

"She cried and then asked about you. She knows the whole story after she had seen it on her local news channel."

"Did you tell her we are having a baby?"

"No, I didn't."

"Why the hell not?"

"Tell the truth, I got a bit mad when she gave me a piece of her mind."

"Which was?"

"To forget about revenge for what happened to Mercy."

"What did you say?"

"Told her I wouldn't rest until I kill them all. I told Ellie the same because she also jumped on the same bandwagon."

"I know you, Matt Deal. You need to do what you think is right. You'll find the right way."

"That's the problem, Anna, I keep thinking they might be right. Besides, I have you and the baby to consider."

"Come here and kiss me, Matt Deal."

"Before I do, I almost forgot something else. It's been a long day. Pat? Is he gay?"

Wolfie laughed loudly. "Kidding me, right? He, Randy and Sean are or were the baddest-assed straight guys... they were special forces... why do you ask?"

"Nothing really, I thought the way he reacted at the graveside was a tad strange, not to mention his hand on my leg. Was he ever touchy-feely with you?"

"Never."

"Okay, asking is all."

I stayed with Anna for another hour before she insisted I go get some sleep. It was a short taxi ride to a nearby Circle Six motel, and I paid and tipped the driver.

My cell phone vibrated as I was thinking of turning in for the night and in a tired remote reflex, I answered, "Hello, Deal here."

"Brendan O'Rourke. You wish know where he is?" The man spoke imperfect English in what sounded like a Mexican accent.

"Who is this?"

"No importa. ¿Quieres saber… o no?"

"Yo no hablo español," I said in a terrible effort at Spanish.

"I said, never mind. Do you want to know… or not?" the Spanish speaking man said.

I wanted to ask him how he got my cell number, then thought better of it as it can be discovered by anyone if they are determined to know it. Instead, I said, "Si, shoot," as I grabbed the hotel notepad and pen, then he gave me the name of a hotel in Texas. I said, "Okay, right. It's San Luis Resort, Galveston, Texas. Is that correct?"

The caller hung up.

Now I was wide-awake and hit speed dial on my cell. "Ellie, sorry, I know it's late, but this is important." Steele was still sleepy, probably dreaming of Mike Diaz, so she took a few moments to register it was me, but I knew she had heard the urgency in my voice. I told her about my call and asked her to check some flights.

"I'll get back to you as soon as I can," Steele said before hanging up.

Thirty minutes later, I answered my cell when I saw Ellie's caller ID appear. "Great, thanks. Delta three-one-five, one pax O'Rourke B, arriving Galveston at 10:00 AM Thursday the ninth," I said writing down the information.

CHAPTER TWELVE

WHERE'S DEAL?

About the same time as Deal arrived at his motel, Bobby Peters and his grandma had just finished eating supper when Bobby heard Sheba, Wolfie's dog, yelp somewhere out in the yard. Before going out to look, he picked up the Glock Deal had given him, making sure there was one in the chamber, and flicked the safety off.

"Be careful," Grandma said.

"Probably Sandy coming back from her night class, but Grandma, please make sure the yard light is switched on and stay away from the door and windows," Bobby said.

Outside in the yard, he saw what had caused Sheba to yelp. A man was holding a taser aimed at the one-eyed dog. That was the last thing Bobby saw until he regained consciousness inside his

Grandma's living room. He knew he was sitting on an armchair, and his wrists and ankles were bound with plastic zip ties. He could also sense the mother of all headaches brewing inside his skull.

Managing to scope the rest of the room, he could see his grandma tied up on the sofa with duct tape smeared across her mouth. He couldn't see the two expressionless big guys standing behind the couch, holding 9-millimetre guns. A voice behind him, *a New Jersey or New York accent*, he thought, said, "Where's Deal?"

Bobby didn't know, and if he did, he would not tell these hoodlums. "I have no idea."

"Okay," the gruff voice said as the third hoodlum stepped in front of Bobby, "You wanna see Grandma here tortured?"

Bobby shook his head.

"Or you prefer we wait for the pretty one to come home after we cut Grandma? *Capiche?*"

Italian Americans, the New Jersey Mob after Matt, Bobby thought. But still he shook his head. "I don't know!" he shouted. "Leave us the fuck alone!"

"Bring the freakin dog in. He can see for himself what's gonna happen if he plays this the wrong way," Gruff voice said, indicating with his pistol to one of the other goons.

One of the two big guys stepped outside for a moment, returning with the carcass of Sheba wrapped in a plastic sheet. He let the plastic shroud drop onto the living room carpet with a thud to be expected from a dog weighing about seventy pounds. Bobby could see the slash wounds across the dog's neck and the blood that had collected inside the shroud. Gruff voice spoke again. "How d'ya like that? Fucking mutt."

Bobby, trying hard to avert his gaze, said, "Look, mister. I know who you are, and I know you're serious. The problem is you are not listening. I do not know where Matt is."

"Cut the old lady." Gruff voice once more nodded towards the same guy who had brought Sheba inside. Without a sound, he walked over to Bobby's Grandma, removed a switchblade from his jacket pocket, pushed back her hair and sliced off her left ear. Bobby couldn't hear her full scream as it was muffled by the duct tape over her mouth, but he watched helplessly as Grandma seemed to faint as she rolled over to her right, resulting in a grotesque pastiche of a sleeping elderly lady.

"Where is he?" Gruff voice repeated.

"Help! Someone help. Call 911," Bobby yelled.

"You know what, guys. I believe him. He has no idea where Deal is," Gruff voice said. He looks right into Bobby's eyes and shot him twice through the head. Turning to Grandma, he repeated the same sequence – a double-tap execution.

Before leaving the house, Gruff voice made a call on his cell. "Done but they don't know where he is."

"Okay. I'll call the Mexicans and get them to dangle the bait," Mike Russo said and hung up.

CHAPTER THIRTEEN

TERRIBLE NEWS

I woke up in my motel room to the sound of my cell ringing. Sleepily I said, "What time is it?" On glancing at the caller ID, I saw it was Elaine Steele.

"Four in the morning. Matt, some terrible news. The Destin cops found Bobby and his grandma dead. Killed pro-style. Two slugs to the head, and the dog's dead too. Not only that, but Lorey and her husband were executed in their home in Miami. Sounds like Lorey was tortured. It must be because they want to know where you are."

"They? You mean Russo?"

"Not sure. I got a call from Mike Diaz telling me two Mexican drug cartel sicarios had flown to Miami, and their speciality is torturing people for information. That's what seems to have happened with Lorey."

"Mike Diaz?"

"Yes, I told you. He's the Mexican Army officer I met at Quantico."

"Right, sorry, I forgot. How do you know about Bobby?"

"Destin P.D. called me. They know I'm involved with the Tallahassee shootings and rightly guessed these slayings were connected."

"Sandy?"

"She's okay but in shock, as she came home and found Bobby and Grandma dead."

"Okay. Here's the thing. Get Anna out of that hospital now… this morning. She will tell you where I want her to go to hide out. After that, you will hear from me. Can you hide Sandy someplace?"

"Sure, but where are you going, Matt?"

"Galveston."

"Texas?"

"That's the one."

Mike Russo's drug trafficking activities were stepped up when he climbed into bed with the *Los Zetas* cartel controlled by their leader, known as *El*

Loco. Brendan O'Rourke became a crucial component in the smuggling routes from Mexico into the United States owing to his legitimate business background in real estate and investments. He also owned a large warehouse in Galveston which acted as a drug trafficking distribution hub for cocaine, heroin, crystal meth, and Mexican-manufactured fentanyl.

Russo had no qualms in using O'Rourke as bait to reel in Matt Deal. He swore to his soldiers and the widows of Messina and Caruso that Deal would die a terrible death. Some of El Loco's sicarios had paid a visit to the Miami home of Deal's ex, Lorey, but she knew nothing. Russo's soldiers had also drawn a blank in Destin with Bobby Peters, Deal's gym employee, but Russo knew with certainty Deal would arrive in Galveston to confront O'Rourke. That was why Russo had to enlist the help of *El Loco* as Galveston was a mere five-hundred mile, eight-hour drive from Monterrey. It was closer to the Mexican cartel's turf than Russo's East Coast turf. Moreover, *El Loco* and his *sicarios* enjoyed killing. His men would also enjoy the fine dining and attractions of the San Luis Resort in Galveston.

I decided I wanted to drive to Galveston. After all, it was a similar trip to that of Galveston to

Monterrey at one hundred miles and one hour long. I needed space after the shocking news of the murders of my friends. I needed thinking time. *Is Celia right? Is Ellie right? Should I stop right now, turn around and be back safe in Anna's arms? Think of our baby, that's right, think of your unborn baby. Make sure the same fate as Mercy's doesn't befall him or her. How else can I protect it without killing all this scum? Mercy, if you can hear me, tell me what to do, please. It's Daddy.*

The satellite radio switched itself on at that thought. It played the Dixie Chicks' *Goodbye Earl* about killing an abusive husband. I listened to the lyrics. *The bastards deserved it*, I thought. *Thanks for the message, Mercy, I love you.*

Two of El Loco's sicarios were checked in at the San Luis Resort when Deal pulled into the parking lot. They were under orders to do nothing… yet… just wait until Deal arrived. They had Deal's photo and description – a red-haired gringo, six feet-two inches tall. Mexicans love nicknames so Deal became known as Chucky, the demonic doll in the film of that name, owing to his red hair. Two pairs of eyes were watching Deal as he checked in at the front lobby.

After I checked in at the front lobby, I made my way to the sixth floor using the elevator. On reaching my room, I decided to freshen up before calling Anna. After my shower, I called her. "Anna, I'm here in the San Luis Resort. How are you?"

"Okay, I guess, but I would be much better if I was there too."

"I know, baby, I know."

"Want a surprise?" Anna said.

"What? Over the phone?"

"I'm here with Pat."

"What? Where?"

"Here at the resort."

"What the hell?"

"Matt, don't get mad. After what happened to Bobby, his grandma, and poor, poor Sheba, it's not safe in Destin, and I need to be near you. Pat said he'd drive so here we are. What room are you in? We just got here."

"Six-thirty-one," I said flatly.

CHAPTER FOURTEEN

SIX-THIRTY-ONE

"You sure he's going to be okay with this?" Pat said.

"He'll be pissed at first, but then he'll calm down," Wolfie said.

"Okay, I'll check in then. I'll ask for the room next to six-thirty-one."

"Cool," Wolfie said.

Following a successful check-in, Pat and Wolfie made their way to the bank of elevators, pinged the button, and exited onto the luxury carpet of the resort's sixth floor. Outside room six-thirty-two, Pat said, "I'll be with you two in five minutes. I think it best if you have a private talk first without me there."

"Good idea," Wolfie said as Pat used the electronic fob to enter his room, set his bag down, and freshen up.

I was ready waiting at the door to my room six-thirty-one when I heard the knock. I opened the door to see Anna standing there, and she reacted to my smile, which was as wide as a twenty-lane highway, with a smile of her own. "Get in here," was all I said, gently taking her arm and guiding her inside the spacious room.

"Bag," Anna said, holding up her backpack.

"First this," I said, kissing her long and hard on the lips.

"Wow! You did miss me. I thought you were going to be pissed at me for just turning up here."

"I was… for a second… then thought I'd rather have you here than hiding away in our bunker."

"And you're okay with Pat being here?"

"We'll see. You need to freshen up after the drive?"

"Later, I'm too excited. Is it okay if Pat joins us? He's in the room next door."

"Yeah, use the hotel phone right there," I said, pointing to a cream coloured telephone next to the enormous flatscreen TV.

I opened the door again a few moments later to allow Pat into the room once I heard the knock. He had only taken a few paces when I said abruptly, "Whose idea was it to follow me to Galveston and Anna, how the hell did you know I was here?" I was asking both if the truth be known.

"My idea and it was Ellie who told me. I told Pat, and he volunteered to drive me here," Anna said.

"We didn't mean to get you mad," Pat added. "I figured it would be safer for Wolfie to be with you rather than hiding out in the Florida woods."

I thought, *At least he's respectful. No one else calls Wolfie Anna except for Ellie and me. I like that, and so does Anna, I guess.* "You could be right, but I'm not sure about the safer bit. Do you know why I'm here?"

"Ellie told me. Brendan O'Rourke is due in town," Anna said.

"Not just in town. He has a reservation in this resort."

"She also told me about the phone call that led you here, from the Mexican or I assume he is Mexican," Anna said. "Don't you think it may be a trap?"

"I do, and that's why I came prepared," I said. "Take a look in that bag, and Anna, while you're there get one of the Glock .45s. I gave yours to

Bobby. Pat, you look too, I want you to know you could be getting into the *Fight at the OK Corral.*"

Pat and Anna stepped over to the large canvas bag at the bottom of the closet. Pat unzipped it and looked inside. "Looks like a small arsenal to me. Small but powerful. Glock pistols, Uzis, binoculars and some grenades but no RPG for me." Pat laughed, easing the tension.

"You both want to stay? I asked.

"I'm not leaving you, Matt," Anna said.

"Unanimous decision," Pat said, still examining the bag's contents. "What's this? It seems a bit underwhelming mixed in with the rest of the armoury," he added, holding up a snub-nosed revolver.

"Pass it over, Pat, that's my backup weapon," I said. Pat handed me the revolver, so I spun the chamber to check it was loaded then closed it, snapped on the safety and tucked it in my waistband at the small of my back. "Okay. That's that then. You both want to stay. Here's the thing. This could get real nasty, so tonight we all relax, have a drink, eat some good food. Tomorrow is another day."

"Sounds good, but I'm not going to be a party-pooper. I'll do my own thing and let you two guys have some time alone," Pat said.

After a few hours of lovemaking and a refreshing shower together, Anna and I ventured out of the hotel, heading for Galveston Harbor where we took a two-hour sunset cruise aboard a twin-engine open-air tour boat. It was a BYOB job, so we picked up a six-pack and a bottle of sparkling wine to take aboard.

During the relaxing cruise, I turned the conversation around to Pat once more. Something was bothering me about him, and I didn't know for sure what it was. "Did Sean say anything about the possibility of Pat being gay?"

"You asked me that before. Is it bugging you?"

"No, not really. I don't even know why I'm asking."

"Matt, I believe it is bothering you. Whether he is or not doesn't matter to us, does it? You must remember it wasn't the thing to 'come out' in special forces. I teased Sean once when he said his relationship with Pat was 'magical.' Sean snapped back at me saying, 'If he was queer, they'd kick him out faster than a Big Mac at a Weight Watchers' meeting.'"

We both laughed, causing some other couples to give us the 'who are the crazy people' stare. That made us laugh more.

CHAPTER FIFTEEN

DELAY

The next morning while Anna got showered, I called Elaine Steele to check for any updates on O'Rourke's flight and his resort reservation. Steele told me O'Rourke had changed his flight and accommodation reservation by twenty-four hours, now due in the next day, one day later than the original schedule. Before ending the call – and making sure the shower was still running – I quietly said, "Thanks, Ellie, and by the way, I think you did right to let Anna know about Galveston."

"I know. She has to be with you, Matt. You take care and look after my sister. Did Pat go too?" Elaine said.

"Yes, what do you make of him?"

"What do you mean?" Elaine asked.

"Gay or straight?"

"Ha! What does it matter? You sound like one of those old-time bible-thumpers," she snorted with faux derision down the line.

After Anna was showered and dressed, we all took breakfast in the resort's main dining room. Pat had joined us. Over a second coffee, I broke the news about the delay in O'Rourke's plans. "So, Pat, you can go off and have some fun. Anna and I will do a bit of scoping the area disguised as a sightseeing trip. It might pay off to get familiar with the neighbourhood."

"I think I'll chill by the pool and let you two lovebirds do your thing," Pat said.

Anna, unable to resist, patted her tummy. "Too late, it is already on the way."

"It?" I said.

"Yeah, it. He or she, I don't want to know yet."

"Right, I'll see you guys later," Pat said.

"Okay, see you. Anna and I will take a taxi to tour the town," I said as I waved Pat cheerio.

The concierge called the appropriately named Yellow Cab Company using a prearranged code given to him by the sicarios who, following instructions, watched every move made by Deal. Within seconds the cab driver was at the front entrance. He jumped out and opened the rear passenger doors to let Deal and Wolfie settle into the air-conditioned interior.

"Where to?" the driver asked, speaking with a Mexican accent. It reminded me of the anonymous phone call leading to this trip to Galveston but dismissed the thought as stupid, reminding myself there must be thousands of men of Mexican descent living in the United States.

"The sights, all of them," I said.

"Tourist places?"

"All places, but skip the business district and the harbour, please. We are relocating here and want to know the area inside out – the good and the bad," I said.

"I show you bad first. Keep your doors locked and the windows up." Enrique Martinez was the driver's name according to the identity badge displayed in the front of the cab. He said nothing as he drove his fares around a city he knew well. He was a second-generation immigrant.

I saw a sign for 26th Street. It wasn't difficult to see we were entering a rundown area judging by the graffiti and many Latino youngsters hanging on street corners. Anna nudged me to draw my attention to an SUV parked in a side street. It was black with blacked-out windows. It didn't belong.

"Probably stolen," I said, but on turning around to look back, I saw it was following the taxi along the two-lane thoroughfare. Instinctively, I patted my holster for reassurance. "Anna, keep your purse open and ready for quick access," I said, knowing where she was carrying her Glock. I was beginning to regret I'd left my backup gun in the bag at the hotel room because my sixth sense was kicking in. The driver appeared oblivious to the tail, if that was what it was. I decided to force myself to stop turning back to get a better view through the rear window.

A few moments after the decision, the black SUV appeared alongside the taxi. It seemed to linger for a time, keeping the same speed as the taxi, until the front passenger's window powered down. "Get down, Anna," I shouted. She did. Before the SUV accelerated away, I could see two smartly dressed young Mexican men inside the vehicle, and they were laughing.

"What was that about?" Anna said.

"They were either fooling around, or they are sicarios, drug cartel assassins. Driver, let's get out of here and find a quieter neighbourhood."

Mr Martinez still said nothing but carried on driving east towards downtown Galveston.

"Anna, as soon as he reaches a safe part of town, you should go back to the resort, this is all a bit scary." I had hardly finished speaking when the same SUV appeared from a side street and stopped sideways in front of the taxi. I whipped my head around on hearing tyres screech behind me. It was another expensive SUV, but white, that had blocked the cab in by pulling up behind.

The taxi driver braked to a sudden halt, throwing Anna and me forward towards the back of the taxi's front seats. "Anna, go now. Run and shoot to kill if you have to. I'll come to find you."

Without protest or hesitation, Anna opened the rear door and ran fast down a side alley. I knew she trusted me.

"Mister Martinez, I'm sorry, but I need your taxi. It's me they want, not you." There was no argument from the driver as he walked away, watched by the sicarios. His job was done.

I got behind the driver's wheel and fumbled for my cell phone. Glancing down I could see Pat's number freshly inputted to speed dial. I tried it four times and got no answer.

CHAPTER SIXTEEN

JAMIE

Pat's cell rang four times while he was swimming in the resort pool. He was having fun with a newfound friend by the name of Jamie. They seemed to click. She was younger than Pat, about twenty-six, and said she was half Thai and half American, her father having married her Thai mother during his United States Air Force service when he was stationed in Thailand. She liked Pat's maturity and good manners, and in turn, Pat enjoyed her carefree ways and unbridled joy for living.

He told her he didn't care she was flat-chested and wasn't bothered that her urchin hairstyle made her look boyish after she put herself down when talking about her looks. Pat disagreed and complimented Jamie on her hairstyle, especially the way it tapered at the back, accentuating her long, delicate neck. He reassured her, telling Jamie she looked fabulous everywhere in her bright red bikini and he truly meant it. They laughed and frolicked for hours in the pool.

There were many things Jamie did not tell Pat. She was scared he may run off after misunderstanding her life story and her predicament. She had no desire to say to him she came into this life as James but was known as Jimmy to everyone in Del Rio, Texas. Her father worked at the nearby Laughlin Air Force Base as a recruiter following his retirement from the United States Air Force, until the day he killed her mother. They had been arguing… again… about Jimmy as her father insisted on calling *his son*. He just couldn't wrap his head around his progeny feeling more woman than a man. This had been going on since Jamie was fourteen. She was sixteen on the day her mother was murdered, beaten to a pulp by a man incapable of understanding that sometimes nature takes its course. Battered to death by a powerfully strong Afro-Caribbean man married to a small, slim Thai woman. Happy Sixteenth Birthday Jamie! And some!

That event was something Jamie felt she couldn't survive, but she did. It was far worse than the bullying at high school. That was bullying from kids who were just as ignorant as her father. At sixteen, Jamie decided Del Rio was not for her, so she fled to the safety of her aunt's home in Alice, Texas. Her Aunt Bessie was her mother's sister. She understood Jamie just like her mother did. After all, transgender people, or ladyboys as they were often called, were commonplace in Thailand as in many Asian countries. Her aunt gave her a home and a refuge. From there, she started planning the rest of her life, but always suffered from the heartache of thinking no man would ever contemplate a serious relationship with her owing to what she did not possess, unlike normal women.

That was when she decided if she couldn't do serious, then she would do one-night stands and plenty of them. And, if she were going to do that, why not make it pay so she could afford surgery procedures to make her womanlier. She found work in a crappy dive of a bar in Corpus Christi where she entertained sailors from all over the world, who were mostly too drunk to navigate their way around Jamie's naked flesh or didn't care. She made good money, with her most significant business outlay being condoms and regular health checks.

Tiring of prostituting herself, Jamie made a concerted effort to see if she could live as a man. Using her Thai passport showing her gender as male, she hatched a mad plan to join the Thai Army. It took two years for her colleagues to suspect *he* was a man who wanted to be a woman and felt way more comfortable as *she* than *he*. Vowing to be true to her real feelings, she returned to Aunt Bessie in Texas, and with her savings started a series of surgical procedures to change her into the beautiful mixed-race person Pat was falling for. She only desired some happiness in her life as Jamie, *not James or Jimmy. She* had left *him* behind when *she* was fourteen.

CHAPTER SEVENTEEN

TRAPPED

Anna saw the narrow alley was blocked at the other end. One of the sicarios was standing at the far side, holding a sawn-off shotgun. She knew she was out of range but started to take her Glock from her purse when she heard a man behind her. *I'm trapped and can't make it out*, she thought.

Turning around, she saw it was another hired assassin. He said with a heavy Mexican dialect, "*Princesa*, don't do anything stupid. I don't like killing ladies, but some of my *compas* do. Give me the gun, and I'll take you to your boyfriend."

I'm between a rock and a hard stone, I can't run. If I shoot, one of them will kill me. Strange, he has kind eyes for a killer.

"Take me to him," Wolfie said, handing over the Glock to the kind-eyed cartel killer.

Frantic was the word that sprang to mind. Yeah, I was agitated. I had no idea if Anna had escaped and if she had, clueless if she was on her way to Pat and the resort. I sized up the situation and couldn't figure out how I was going to drive away with the two SUVs blocking my front and rear. I saw Mr Martinez still hanging around, shrugging at the sight in front of him, but he ran off after one of the sicarios yelled, "¡Conduce, vete a la mierda!" *I've got a good idea what that meant.*

My attention was now on a white van with sliding doors that just pulled up behind the SUV blocking me at the rear. Four guys jumped out, and I knew this was deep shit. I was now surrounded by eight sicarios, all Mexican by their looks. The two meanest looking hombres were dressed in smart, lightweight suits, no neckties, and bulges under the jackets covering up their weapons. They were also both the youngest in appearance with shaven heads. *They seem like twin brothers*, I thought.

I knew the other six were also carrying weapons. They were mainly dressed in chinos and wearing black leather jackets. They appeared older than the two new arrivals.

Fight or flight? I could sense the adrenaline coursing through my body. One of the twins pulled out a gun but didn't point it at me. Instead, he gestured for one of the older men to approach the taxi. In doing so, the older guy withdrew a 9-millimetre gun from his waistband and with the free hand, knocked on the driver's window, gesturing for me to get out.

Gripping my Glock, I opened the door with a violent swing, catching the older guy across the knees. Seizing the initiative, I jumped to my feet and cracked my gun down hard on the sicario's head. Two more of the older men ran at me, guns ready. I used all the speed of my Muay Thai and silat training, kicking one in the groin, forcing him to his knees while chopping at the other's neck. One was now vomiting, holding his testicles, the other gasping for air, clutching his throat. Another sicario approached with his gun aimed at me. The fight was interrupted by one of the twins shouting, "No. Don't shoot. We take him alive." He had seen what I had not.

The kind-eyed killer was bringing Wolfie over, dragging her roughly by the arm until she bit down on his hand. "*Pinche puta!*" he yelled in pain, drawing my attention to Anna's reappearance.

The twin shouted at me again in accented English, "Drop the gun, and your *puta* lives."

Think Deal, think. I slowly walked a few paces to the taxi, starting to place my gun on the roof, but instead, I pulled out my cell. Shielded from view, I speed dialled Pat. The call was answered. I had to be quick, and I was. "Pat, don't talk. Wolfie and I are captured… about to be taken… sicarios… go hide as they will come for you too and call Elaine Steele." I then dropped the phone on the ground. Stamping on it, I made sure only fragments remained.

Now surrounded by the sicarios, the twin giving the orders took my gun from the car roof. Placing my Glock in his waistband, he struck me twice across the head with his pistol, forcing me to the ground. I heard Anna cry out, "Leave him be. You have us now." It was a useless plea. The twins started kicking me as I lay prone on the road. I remember being kicked for about two minutes. Then I stopped moving.

"Oh, my God! You've killed him," Anna sobbed as two of the older sicarios roughly shoved her to the van with the sliding doors. As the door was closing, she could see Matt being lifted off the ground by some of the other thugs. A few moments later, the door opened again when Matt was bundled unconscious into the van alongside her. At gunpoint, the kind-eyed killer tied them up with heavy-duty zip ties and placed duct tape across their mouths. Neither Anna nor Deal were able to move or call out. She could only watch with fearful wide eyes as two syringes were plunged into first her arm and then Matt's. Before she lost consciousness, she heard the convoy of the two SUVs and the van accelerating away from the scene and the sensation of speed made her feel like vomiting. *Where are we going, what's going to happen to us?* Anna thought as she passed out.

CHAPTER EIGHTEEN

FRIEND OR NOT?

As soon as Deal ended the call, Pat left the pool and began thinking about the best course of action. *Go hide… sicarios, Deal said.*

"Who was that?" Jamie said.

"Huh? Nobody, nothing."

Jamie, sensing trouble, threw on a sarong before collecting her bag. She followed Pat as he headed for the main resort building, concerned at his reaction to this call. Pat took the elevator to his room with Jamie in close tow. "What is it?" she repeated several times on the way up.

"I told you, nothing."

"Funny nothing that freaks you out. Am I a friend or not?"

"Yes, but it would be best if you stay out of this. It might be scary."

"I like scary," she said.

"Okay, but do everything I tell you. If you can do that, you're my friend." Pat thought, *This is scary, and I have no right to ask her anything, but she seems capable. Who knows, she may even be an asset.*

"Yes, sir," Jamie said, throwing a mock salute.

Entering his room, Pat said, "Jamie, just sit on the bed and don't say or do a thing unless I ask you to."

"How exciting, is this one of those sex games?"

"No. And you already broke the rules. Now shut up."

Hmm, this is creepy, she thought. *Should I go?*

Jamie watched Pat's every movement. She wasn't surprised to see him take an automatic pistol out of the closet safe. Holding the gun ready, Pat first checked the large bathroom, then back to the expansive double closet, scanning inside for goodness know what, she thought. Satisfied, he turned to the balcony screen doors, opened them and walked outside. He disappeared for a while, but she jumped off the bed on hearing a clatter outside.

On venturing out onto the balcony, she saw Pat had knocked over a trash can. "What happened?" Jamie said.

"I knocked it over climbing back from Deal's room."

"Deal?"

"Yeah, my friends I was telling you about. Well, he's Matt Deal, and his lady is called Wolfie."

"Strange name."

"Her real name is Anna, but she likes strangers to know her as Wolfie."

"So why were you on their balcony?"

"To see if their screen door was open."

"Why?"

"Jamie, you're not sticking to the rules. Some heavy stuff is going down here, and it is dangerous. If you want to go, go right now otherwise be quiet, let me think and just do as I tell you."

"Sorry, Pat. I'll stay. I might be crazy, but I like you… I trust you too."

"Okay, follow me. I'm going back."

Jamie followed him out onto the balcony as instructed when she heard Pat say, "Get down!"

"What is it?" she whispered.

"A bunch of guys arrived in two SUVs and were scoping the upper balconies. They could be looking for me."

"I think it's a good time for you to tell me what the heck's going on."

"You're right, and I should have told you before. Deal and Wolfie have been taken."

"Taken?"

"Yeah, captured. Deal called me. All he said was 'go hide' and mentioned Mexican cartel sicarios."

"That was the call at the pool?"

"Yeah, now you know why I was reluctant to tell you. I'm scared too, and that doesn't happen often."

"Where are you going to hide?"

"Inside the closet in Matt's room. It's big, and I'm hoping they will never think of me hiding so close to my room."

"*Us*. Not me or I. *Us*. Let me take a peep. They're not expecting a woman."

Before Pat could prevent her, Jamie looked over the balcony parapet. "Clear," she said.

They climbed over onto Matt's balcony, opened the screen doors and went straight for the closet. They lay there in the darkness, heartbeats hammering until the noise of loud banging disturbed the peace of the sixth floor. Pat placed his finger on Jamie's lips in a shushing gesture. He was surprised and excited when she lightly kissed and then sucked it.

The banging noise stopped but was replaced by a man's shout. "Drop your weapons." Pat thought, *That's cops.* Several shots were fired then silence.

Pat and Jamie felt frozen in time as they clung to each other for what seemed like thirty minutes. Figuring whoever had fired the shots had left, Pat thought it was safe to venture out to the hall. He was not too surprised to see three uniformed hotel security guards lying dead or dying in pools of blood on the carpeted hall outside room six-thirty-two. On a closer look, he could see the door of his room had been forced open and his belongings strewn over the place.

Turning to Jamie, he said, "Time to go. Are you still with me?"

She squeezed his hand, saying, "Try to stop me."

"One thing to do, I have to get a bag from Matt's room."

CHAPTER NINETEEN

PRISONERS

The van stopped. The windows were tinted so no one could see in, but the occupants could see out. I felt cold water splashed on my face. I was drowsy, I guess I had been drugged with a strong sedative but relieved to find Anna alive and right next to me. Plastic ties were bound to our wrists and ankles making movement impossible. I also sensed my mouth had been taped. Anna confirmed this and told me the duct tape must have been removed once we were unconscious. We checked each other out, and I was thankful to see Anna looking unhurt.

Anna spoke softly. "You okay? Your head is smeared with blood. Mind you, it's dried blood."

"I'm fine. What about you?" I said, but my head and ribs hurt like hell.

"Good. Don't worry about me," she said and gave a weak smile.

I could see we were in a sliding-door van, but now two other cartel members were looking down at us. One of them handed over a plastic bottle containing cold water. Despite being prisoners, I was grateful for the drink as their captor held the bottle so we could swallow the cold liquid. The other sicario trained his pistol on us.

"You sure you are okay?" I said.

"Fine, but you look like you're in pain," Anna said.

"Headache for sure, and I think I may have a cracked rib. But we are still alive."

"*Ustedes dos, cállate la boca*," the water carrier said.

"That means shut the fuck up," said the other sicario. "I get the feeling *tu no hablas español*, eh?"

"*Si, no hablas español*," Anna said.

I saw the van was parked at a gas station. From the signage, it was clear we were in McAllen, Texas, close to the Mexican border town of Reynosa. *If they want to take us across the border, how the hell they going to do that at a border checkpoint?* The answer came to me immediately. *Drug mule smuggling route.*

I got a confirmation of sorts as soon as the second sicario spoke again. "No talking. We will be switching vehicles soon." That was reinforced a few minutes later when the van left the gas station, but instead of heading due south, the driver went west. I was tied up in the back of this van, so could only stay silent and watch. I saw the signs for Route 83 and Rio Grande City flash by for what I guessed was about forty miles. Then, I saw the Rio Grande City limits sign – population 14,000, then the van stopped again on a dusty side road just past the sign. The rear panel door slid open. The two sicario guards cut our ankle ties before escorting us at gunpoint to our new transport – a huge bright yellow tractor-trailer truck, with a 'Lone Star Trucking Inc.' logo across the driver's door and the side of the trailer. On looking over to my left, I saw the steel structure of the Rio Grande City–Camargo International Bridge joining Texas to Mexico.

The two sicarios walked with us to the back of the trailer where the driver, who appeared to be a white American judging by his look and accent as he spoke briefly to the two Mexicans, operated the hydraulic liftgate. As we were told to climb in, I heard the van set off, closely followed by the black and white SUVs that blocked in the taxi back in Galveston. Once the liftgate reached the same level as the trailer floor, it stopped so I could see rows of wooden pallets filled with shrink-wrapped cardboard boxes. There were about four rows placed neatly at the front of the trailer. Anna and I were told to stand and not move while we watched the driver using a pump handle jack manoeuvre the pallets to make a walkway to the trailer front. Once he had done that, I saw him reach up as if he were looking for something. It was then a metal roller door opened to reveal a secret compartment.

Drugs, people, guns, they could use it for anything they choose, I thought.

The sicarios waved their guns, pointing at the opening. We got into the hiding place with the two thugs for company. The steel door closed, and I heard the driver rearranging the pallets before I listened to the hydraulic whine of the liftgate. The next thing I heard was the throaty rumble of the giant diesel engine growl into life.

The truck rolled smoothly for about ten minutes, but from there on, it was stop-start for another ten. *Must be a line of traffic*, I thought. *No one's going to find us. US Border Patrol only checks incoming, and the Mexicans will let anything in if a bribe is paid.* That thought made me feel despondent.

"About three hours' drive. We will stop and eat if you promise to behave," one of our captors said.

I heard Anna's stomach rumble. I guessed she was hungry. Responding to the mention of food, Anna tried out her best Spanish and said, "*Si, lo haremos. Tengo hambre.*"

"*Muy bien. Comemos,*" our captor said with a thousand-yard stare directed at me.

I said nothing. My mind was racing.

CHAPTER TWENTY

LAY LOW

"Elaine, it's me, Pat. Matt and Anna's friend. Matt told me to contact you."

"What's happened?"

"Taken by a drug cartel, I think."

"Think?"

"He was and Anna too. Said it was some sicarios and told me to go hide and call you."

"Shit. I knew this O'Rourke tale was likely to be a trap, but that's Matt for you. Hard-headed and impulsive. What else do you know?"

"I saw the sicarios at the San Luis Resort. They were trying to find me. They came up to my room and shot some hotel security guards."

"You okay?"

"Yeah. We got out of there before the cops arrived."

"We?"

"Me and a friend."

"Where are you now?"

"Just outside Galveston. I don't know what to do."

"Here's what you do… nothing. Wait and hide. Lay low. I have a contact in the Mexican Army and I'll see what I can find out. Keep your cell charged. I take it this is the number you're calling from."

"Right. I'll wait to hear back from you."

The call ended. Jamie said, "What did she say?"

"Lay low. Stay off the radar."

"Where?"

"No idea."

"I have an aunt in Corpus Christi. It's not far, and I'm sure she'll let us stay with her. She also has an old pick-up truck she never uses so maybe we can switch. No one will be looking for her truck."

"Jamie, I've only met you today, but I think you are wonderful," Pat said.

"Kiss me," Jamie said.

Elaine Steele hastily dialled the number for her friend Colonel Mike Diaz after a swift but careful consideration of where the kidnappers may be taking Deal and Anna. She got through immediately once Diaz saw who was calling. "Mike, yes, I'm good. Listen, please, I have a delicate situation."

"You got it, Ellie, I'll arrange a tactical unit, and as soon as I hear more from you, we will go in hard. We'll find your friends, don't worry," Diaz said from his base in Nuevo Laredo, Mexico.

In a little over four hours, Jamie had directed Pat to her aunt's gated community home. It was a substantial four-bedroomed home which in truth was now far too large for the aunt's needs since her husband passed. Jamie had Pat promise to tell her aunt they had known each other for much longer than one day. It worked as her aunt, Bessie to give her a name, offered the use of a large bedroom for the couple to sleep in containing a queen bed. It also had a shower room.

After a supper of fried chicken, roasted potatoes and a medley of vegetables, Bessie said goodnight to the couple. It wasn't long before they too were in bed but in their case, for the first time together. They quickly disrobed, each admiring the others' semi-clad body before sampling the comfortable bed. They didn't sleep right away as they engaged in prolonged sensual foreplay.

"You seem nervous," Jamie said.

"It's been a long time," Pat said.

"How long?" she said.

"With a woman? I was a teenager."

Jamie had an instinct. She knew. "I hope you like this then," she said, almost coyly.

After the mutually satisfying sex, Pat said, "That *was* a surprise."

"But you liked it, yes?" Jamie asked.

"Loved it. Let's do it again."

Mike Russo and Brendan O'Rourke changed plans on learning of the shootings at the San Luis Resort. Russo and two of his wise guys flew into Galveston from Newark, New Jersey, hooking up with O'Rourke at a diner near to the resort.

"Any news on Deal's compadre?" Russo said.

"The tall blond guy? Gone. He took off with a woman after the hotel guards were shot by El Loco's men," O'Rourke said.

"What woman?"

"His men asked around. She was around the pool with Deal's pal most of the day. Tallish, slim, short black hair, good body but no boobs. The guy running the pool bar said she was a looker but a bit boyish. He didn't have a name for her. She was on a day entry ticket."

"Right, where are we gonna get a car? Can't take this airport rental across the border," Russo said.

"I'll take care of that. Let me make a call," O'Rourke said.

Thirty minutes later, Russo, his two wise guys, and O'Rourke were heading for the border in an SUV commandeered from O'Rourke's general manager at the Galveston warehouse.

CHAPTER TWENTY-ONE

ENMOLADA

The yellow tractor-trailer pulled up at a quiet roadside cantina, a kind of Mexican truck stop, where the driver reversed the process of secreting the four people hidden in the covert compartment. Before getting out, one of the sicarios said, "You are now deep in Mexico, near Monterrey. I will cut your ties, but if you try anything at all, we will also cut your throats. You, gringo, Chucky, you hear me?"

I said, "I hear you." What else was there to say?

The sicario touched Anna's face, drawing a line from her cheek to her top lip with his finger. "Good, because if you let me down your *puta* will be sold as a piece of meat at *el burdel* for men to play with as they desire, but maybe after I try her first."

"We hear you, don't we, Matt?"

"Loud and clear. Just untie us," I said. Play it cool, and I might get a chance to kill the creep.

After the ties were cut and we were all out of the trailer, the truck driver got back into the cab and drove off, disappearing out of view down the highway with only the occasional dark smoke plume drifting skyward from the stack as the truck started climbing a mountain section. I took in the scenery, including the police car parked outside the cantina, and waited for instructions. "We go in. Ignore the cops in the car, they work for us," one of the sicarios said.

With one sicario in front, the other in the rear, Anna and I walked to the cantina front doors. As we passed the police car, the cop in the driver's seat wound down the window and gave a cheery, "Hola," to the sicarios who simply nodded in his direction but didn't speak. I thought, *They must have the entire provincial police on the payroll.*

All four of us went inside the cantina, and despite the circumstances I enjoyed a meal of enmolada, a rolled corn tortilla filled with shredded chicken and cotija cheese. Anna seemed to enjoy it too. We were hungry. The sicarios also ordered cold sodas which were refreshing. A couple of locals were the only other customers, and they ignored our gringo presence and that of the two sicarios. They knew to stay out of cartel business, as did the local police. The meal was taken in utter silence, only broken at the end when the sicario called over to the waitress so he could pay for the food. As soon as she scooped up the money laid on the table, the sicario said, "Let's go."

Anna and I followed them outside where the quieter of the two sicarios pulled out a car key fob from his trouser pocket, pressed it, and I heard the unlock blip of a car security system. Looking towards the sound, I saw a sliding door van like the one used to transport us to the border, but this bore Mexican plates. "Get in," the sicario said.

We did as we were told, with Anna and I slipping into the first row of the rear seats while the two Mexicans climbed into the front seats, the quieter one taking the wheel. On starting the engine, the talkative one swung around to point his gun at us through the wire mesh separating the front from the rear seats. "Be good. We will get there soon."

"Where are we going?" I said as I tried the door handle out of sight of our captor. It was locked.

"You will see soon."

"Why are Mexicans involved in kidnapping us? We have no grudge with you," I added.

"I suppose it does no harm as you will find out soon enough. Your enemies work closely with our boss. He is doing them a favour."

"Who is your boss?" I said.

"You know him as *El Loco*. To me, he is *el jefe*."

"The chief?" Anna said.

"Si, the chief. The boss."

"I thought El Loco was boss of the Los Zetas cartel," Anna said.

"I see you know your Mexican geography, *bella dama*. He lives in Monterrey most of the time."

"Why?" I said encouraged by his apparent newfound openness.

"Turf war. *Guerra por el territorio*. He is closer to the smuggling routes into the United States. The important routes are on his turf, but the Gulf cartel gets other ideas sometimes. That's when *el jefe* makes an example."

"Example?" I asked.

"Decapitation and hangs their heads from bridges. They soon get the message," the Mexican said with a wry smile.

We are as good as dead. Anna, I love you. I'm so sorry, I thought.

I looked at Anna and knew she was thinking something similar. The frown on her forehead was telling me exactly what she was thinking: *We aren't getting out of this alive, and that's why he's telling us this.*

CHAPTER TWENTY-TWO

HACIENDA

The next thirty minutes of the drive was in silence. I saw they were turning into a long road. It was unmade, with potholes, so the van took it easy, attracting the stares of the locals who lived in the makeshift tin-roof shanties on both sides of the track. After a few hundred yards, I saw the large metal gates leading to a cement road and beyond that in the distance a magnificent two-storey hacienda painted all white, with bright red roof tiles.

Three Mexicans were guarding the gates. As soon as they saw the van there was no challenge, but on speaking to the driver, one of them delivered a reminder to take the gringos to one of the outlying adobe-style houses, calling it, " *la sala de tortura.*"

I need not be fluent in Spanish to start comprehending our fate. It took five minutes driving through the sprawling ranch estate to reach a complex of flat-roofed adobe houses lining the road with each one slightly higher than the next. The adobe house with the highest roof was the last, and the van stopped outside. All four of us alighted. The sicarios, guns drawn, escorted Anna and me inside the building. We could see this house was empty with several separate rooms all on one storey. On glancing into one of the areas, I saw a metal bar festooned with heavy metal chains. *The torture room?* I surmised. We were then hustled into a small back room. It was empty, with no furniture, and had pipes crisscrossed over the wall with a single small slit for ventilation. The room stunk of stale tobacco despite the ventilation slit.

The sicario who had done all the talking ordered us to sit with our backs to this wall. Once we had complied, he put fresh plastic zip ties around our ankles and tied one hand to the largest pipe by using another heavy-duty link. Now, we both had one free hand. The sicario placed three bottles of water near us, and before leaving, he said, "No point in shouting. There is no one to help you."

We gave it ten minutes before speaking. "Anna, I've checked out this room, and I can't see any chance of escape. Any ideas?"

"Yes. They never searched me everywhere. There was no intimate search. I have my cell hidden."

"You're kidding me... no, you're not. That's fantastic. Can you call Ellie and Pat?"

Anna wriggled her hand inside her panties, retrieving the cell phone, and with the one free hand speed dialled Elaine Steele. After several minutes she gave up as there was no answer. Then trying Pat on speed dial, he picked up immediately. "Wolfie, is that you?"

"Drop the Wolfie, call me Anna. And, yes, it's me. Now just listen. Matt and I are okay. Make your way to Monterrey, Mexico."

"Where in Monterrey?"

"El Loco's hacienda, in a small adobe house on the estate. Just find it and one other thing... bring the bag of weapons Matt told you to get from our room."

"I got them and on my way. You want I should tell Elaine Steele?"

"Yes. And no one calls me. We'll call out when and if we can."

Pat hurriedly recounted the gist of the phone conversation to Jamie. She insisted she should join him.

"No, Jamie. This is way too risky."

"I can shoot, and I do unarmed combat," Jaimie said.

"Where did you learn that?"

"Long story, I'll tell you once we rescue your friends."

"Better use Aunt Bessie's truck," Pat said, even more curious about this mystery person. "I'll call Elaine Steele on the way south."

"Who is she?"

"Special Agent, FBI and Matt's friend. They used to be detectives together in England. I'll get you up to speed on the journey. I take it you have a passport?"

CHAPTER TWENTY-THREE

MONTERREY

After only thirty minutes of driving, Pat called Elaine Steele with Matt's news. She, in turn, relayed the information to Mike Diaz, who couldn't believe his luck at the mention of El Loco.

It took Pat just over six hours to cover the nearly three-hundred miles to Monterrey from Alice, Texas, where Aunt Bessie lived. They crossed the border at Laredo where a perfunctory search of the truck at the checkpoint became more truncated on showing a wad of greenbacks. That was to ensure the border guards didn't search Matt's bag. He stopped once to fuel up the old Toyota pick-up truck and grab some sandwiches to eat on the move.

Daylight was breaking as they neared Monterrey and they could see the imposing black mountains surrounding the town. On spotting them, Jamie said, "Jeez! They are scary, man."

Pat thought, *You're right. Scary and creepy.* "Right, tell me if you see a likely place. It will stand out like a sore thumb. It will be the fanciest and very conspicuous, probably surrounded by shacks and poorer places. Anna said the main house was white, two-storeys, and a bunch of small adobe houses somewheres on the ranch."

"Copy that," Jamie said.

Pat was tempted to probe into her background at that point. *Copy that… I can shoot and do unarmed combat,* he thought. *What else don't I know about her? She'll tell me in her own good time.*

"I can ask a local if you like," Jamie said.

"You speak Spanish?"

"Enough to get by. Let me practise… *Hola, estoy buscando una gran casa blanca de dos pisos y un montón de pequeñas casas de adobe en algún lugar del rancho.*"

"Sounds good to me," Pat said.

Ten minutes later, it worked as they spied a local woman walking along the road. "Hello, I am looking for a big white house, two-storeys, and a bunch of small adobe houses somewhere on the ranch," Jamie said in fluent Spanish.

The woman replied, "*Sí, a cuatro millas de aquí se llega a un camino de tierra, gira allí. No te puedes perder la casa.*"

"*Muy buena gracias,*" Jamie said smiling.

"What does that mean?" Pat said.

"Very good, thank you."

"Not that, the long bit," Pat said, laughing.

"Yes, four miles from here you come to a dirt road, turn there. You can't miss the house. "

"Let's go," Pat said, still laughing.

The frivolity was cut short when Pat's cell rang. He saw it was Anna's number.

"Pat, it's Matt. Just listen because we never know when someone will walk in. Answer me after I finish. Once you locate the adobe houses, you must get on a roof, drop a flash-bang grenade through the skylight and I will call you to tell you how close you are to us. You got the flash-bangs in the bag?"

"Yes. Twelve stuns and three live. And we are near now."

"Great. We? You and Jamie?"

"Yeah. You have a problem with that?"

"No, man, that's on you. "

The call ended.

"Hide it. I can hear footsteps outside," I said. Anna thrust the cell phone back down her panties, first switching it off to preserve battery life.

The door opened wide, and three men entered. Two looked like Americans dressed in business suits. The third appeared to be Mexican, dressed flamboyantly in cowboy attire complete with fancy leather boots.

The smaller of the two Americans walked over to me and kicked me in the face. "What the fuck and who the fuck are you?" I spat through bloody lips and a broken tooth.

"You remember a kid called Conor O'Rourke?"

"Yeah. I killed the piece of shit." The man kicked me again, but harder. I felt a bone in my nose crack.

"Where are my manners?" he said. "I'm Brendan O'Rourke, the father of the boy you murdered." He pulled a photo out of his jacket inside pocket. "There, take a good look at his face. The face you saw in the Atlanta bar the night you and your one-eyed bitch shot him dead in the restroom."

"What do you want from me?" I said. "If it's an apology, you can go fuck yourself. Your son and his frat friends put my daughter in a coma after gang-banging her. For god's sake, she was fifteen."

"We don't give a fuck about that, do we Mike?"

"Let me guess," Anna said, "the hoodlum from New Jersey. Give our best to Messina and Caruso, *won't cha.*" I gave out a weird little laugh at Anna's take on a Jersey hoodlum accent. That was soon stifled as Mike Russo leaned towards Anna, drew back his hand and slapped her hard across the face causing a gash with his diamond-studded pinkie ring.

"You will both die a slow and excruciating death. I promise you. My friend here has experts to carry it out as I watch," Russo said, gesturing to the Mexican cowboy, AKA El Loco, the cartel boss.

"I will watch you both suffer," O'Rourke said as they left the room laughing, "and enjoy every moment."

CHAPTER TWENTY-FOUR

COPS

Pat drove on towards the dirt track mentioned by the local woman. He had been going for a few minutes when Jamie spotted what they were looking for. "That must be it. Pull in here."

Pat saw it too. A long dirt road lined with makeshift tin-roofed shanties. He stopped at the entrance to the track before retrieving the binoculars from Matt's bag.

Focussing the field glasses, he saw the white hacienda with its red-tiled roof way beyond the gates guarding the entrance to the ranch estate. Scanning away some distance to the right, he saw the adobe houses. "That's where we need to be," he said, handing the glasses to Jamie.

"How are we going to do that? There's no way past the guards on that gate," she said.

"I'll turn about then carry on down the highway until we see those adobe houses on our left. Maybe we can get closer to them and spring a surprise. Even better, there may not be any guards there."

"What are we waiting for?" Jamie said.

Another few minutes of driving with Jamie acting as the spotter brought them closer to the adobe houses. "There they are," Jamie cried.

"Yeah, I see them. How the fuck do we get closer?" Pat said estimating the houses were set back from the highway about three-hundred yards.

Using the binoculars, Jamie scanned the surrounding fields. "There. Up ahead, there must be a track or something. There's a police car parked up," she said.

"Fucking A! Cops are all we need," Pat said. "No choice, I guess. Let's go and say hello."

Pat found the track, another dusty dirt road and sure enough a gold and green, provincial police car was parked at the end of the trail where a wire fence loomed large to keep out unwanted guests from the hacienda estate. As Pat turned into the track, he handed an Uzi to Jamie. "Do you know how to fire one of these?" he asked then watched in amazement as Jamie broke the weapon down, checked it, then reassembled it in seconds.

"Yes," Jamie said and didn't utter another word.

Who is she? Pat thought and not for the first time since meeting her such a short time ago.

Pat stopped the old Toyota pickup truck short of the police car. There was no movement either inside it or nearby. As Jamie got out of her aunt's car, she pulled down the peak of her forage cap as if to signal she meant business, backed up by her handling the Uzi in a state of readiness. He said quietly, "These guys are probably on the payroll as guards at the vulnerable spots. Be careful." Jamie didn't answer but just flashed him the 'OK' hand signal.

Sneaking up to the police car, Pat looked inside to find two uniformed police officers sleeping. He rapped on the driver's window, aiming his Uzi at the cops until they awoke. Jamie did the same but at the passenger side when she saw a third cop sitting upright in the rear seat and smoking what seemed to be a large marijuana joint. He looked startled on seeing Jamie and on starting to draw his pistol, Jamie fired a short burst, killing the cop instantly. Pat responded by firing a lethal barrage from the Uzi at the two in the front. There were now three dead Mexican cops and an overwhelming aroma of marijuana escaping from the car's interior through the shattered windows.

Pat said on surveying the scene, "Cheech and Chong and *Up In Smoke*, I presume." As Jamie and Pat laughed at this quip as a form of release from nervous tension, neither of them saw the fourth cop in the bushes pulling up his uniform pants after taking a dump. Now serious again, Pat said, "I'll go and get Matt's bag from the truck. Wait here, okay?"

"Yes, I'll take a look at that fence while I'm waiting," Jamie said.

Pat strode off in the direction of the truck which he'd parked some fifty yards away as Jamie lay down her Uzi on the grass next to the fence. She started to survey the wire fence when the fourth cop snuck up behind her. On hearing something he said in Spanish, Jamie wheeled around to face him and the gun he was holding. Silently, she struck like a cobra. On pure instinct and some training, Jamie kicked out with a straight leg, hitting him hard in his groin. Involuntarily releasing his grip on the gun, the cop momentarily gasped for air before retaliating by throwing a right-handed haymaker at Jamie's face. She saw it coming and grasped his wrist, throwing it back at an unnatural angle until she heard the bone snap. The fight was over but not before the returning Pat had witnessed the *coup de grâce* of Jamie disabling the fourth cop before putting one round through his head.

"Where the fuck …" Pat started to ask before Jamie cut him short.

"We can't afford him using the police car radio."

"I meant, where did you learn to fight like that?"

"Never mind. That's a story for later. Now, let's find Matt and Anna. Bring the truck here next to the fence, so we can climb over."

CHAPTER TWENTY-FIVE

TORTURE

Anna and I assessed the situation. "We just got to stay alive until Pat and his friend locate us," I whispered.

"It's the only hope we have," Anna said just as quietly.

"If anyone can rescue us, it'll be him. You know better than anyone that he's a skilled operator, a highly trained special forces combatant."

"What's this about Jamie?" Anna said.

"I trust him to know what he's doing bringing her along."

"Just because she's a woman?" Anna said.

"I don't think this is the right time to talk about that, do you?"

Our conversation was interrupted by the two sicarios who looked like twin brothers, the ones involved in our capture in Galveston. One of them said, "We all go to the next room," as he guarded us with gun drawn while his twin cut the plastic ties.

"Why?" Anna said.

"You will see," the twin holding the gun said. "Walk now." We were taken into the room we saw when we first arrived. There was the bar, a metal bar with heavy metal chains attached to it. It was the room both of us thought could be the torture room. O'Rourke, Russo and El Loco, the cartel leader still in his cowboy attire, were sitting on the far side of the room.

"Meet my experts in torture," El Loco said, "the Hernandez brothers. First, they kill the *puta*... slowly... while you watch, Matt Deal. You will be able to do nothing to save her as her lifeblood trickles from her body. Every drip will tear your heart in two while my friends here enjoy the show. Me? I simply enjoy killing so when the *pinche puta* is dead, O'Rourke will kill you. Nothing personal. It's my favour to my *amigos*."

"You're scum, all of you," I said.

"Mister Deal, your attitude demonstrates you believe help is at hand. Your friends from Galveston, yes?" El Loco said. I said nothing, but my heart sank. "You think I don't know they are here?"

"What are you talking about?" Anna said.

"I am talking about your friend from the resort and his girlfriend. Do not worry, we have plans for them too. After *güero* and his skinny girlfriend are captured, I will sell her skinny ass to the cheapest whorehouse in Mexico where she will be used by many men and become nothing but a piece of meat. Enough talking, tie him up and get the *puta* on the bar," El Loco said.

Struggling was useless, they tied me up with another plastic tie to an eyehole at the end of a metal rod protruding from the bare wall. I could only watch helplessly as the two twins first tied Anna's arms behind her back, then attached heavy chains to her ankles before yanking her up off the ground, so she was now hanging upside down from the bar. Anna kicked and struggled, but the twins were too powerful.

"Now watch this, my friends. This is good," El Loco said, "and don't worry Deal, Javier trained as a medic, so he knows what he's doing. She will bleed out slowly before your own eyes."

On cue, Javier Hernandez withdrew a cloth pouch from his suit jacket, and laying it on the bare table in front of Anna, pulled out a stainless-steel scalpel. Anna's head was suspended about five feet above the room floor. He cut her neck, making four incisions. Blood flowed slowly, forming a small pool drip by drip.

"It can take hours for her to die," El Loco announced with a hint of glee in his tone. "You will watch every drip, Deal, while my friends and I go for a drink and some food at my hacienda. When we get back and when she's dead, O'Rourke will shoot you in the head. If she still breathes, Javier will make more cuts, but to the carotid, so we can all see your *puta* die, *then* you get shot."

El Loco, the Hernandez twins, O'Rourke and Russo left the room laughing and locking the door as they went.

Fuck, I must do something, as I looked into Anna's pleading eyes. She didn't say a word. I guess she was in shock at the horror unfolding, at what was happening.

I thought… quickly… *there must be something.* Glancing all around the room, I finally focussed on my tethered wrist. *Harry Houdini,* I thought, *the great escapologist.* Then concentrating back to Anna, I tried to sound as confident as possible given the circumstances. "Anna, I know this sounds stupid, but you must breathe easy and don't move or struggle. The less blood you lose, the better for your chances. I'm going to try to get free." She made no response.

I took a massive gulp of air, steeling myself for the imminent pain. I seized the thumb of my tethered hand with my free hand and dislocated my thumb. Inside my head, I tried to freeze the searing pain as if it didn't exist. I repeated that but on my index finger alongside the dislocated thumb. Trying my hardest to stifle any noise, I did wince slightly and involuntarily at the waves of pain crashing through the nerves that were intent on sending signals to receptors in my brain. I can't say I enjoy pain, but there's something about its initial heat that triggers my ability to ignore it. Now able to focus, I found I could slide my hand free from the plastic tie. Walking over to Anna, I reached up to her waistband and putting my good hand inside, I located the cell phone, praying there was still battery life and a good signal.

CHAPTER TWENTY-SIX

BLEEDING

"Pat! You gotta get here, pronto. No time to explain. You at the adobe houses yet?" I said.

"Right outside. We were waiting for you to call," Pat said.

"Be careful. They know you and Jaime are here. Start throwing those flash-bangs through the skylights. I'll hear them and know how close you are. If I need to, I'll think of a way of guiding you to us."

"Okay."

I felt around at the chains tied around Anna's ankles and suspending her from the bar. I was relieved to see there was no lock. They were wrapped around her in such a way they held her in place. "Anna, don't talk. I'll try and get you down and out of these chains." Though her head was hanging upside down, I noticed the tears forming in the corners of her eyes. "I'll do it, I promise, and we'll get out of here." I once more blocked out the pain from my injured hand in unravelling the heavy chains. Finally, once they were moved, I took all her body weight on my shoulders and slid her over the bar, letting her drop gently on to her feet. I guided her to one of the chairs vacated by our captors, sat her down, and started to look for something to cut her wrist ties.

BANG!

Right at that moment, I heard a stun grenade explode. *Close*, I thought. I also heard footsteps running away and not towards Anna and me. "That's Pat," I said to reassure Anna.

Resuming my search for something to cut Anna's wrist tie, I remembered the metal rod I had been secured to. I grabbed it and pulling with all my weight, it started to rock in the adobe wall. I thought it would work as these walls are made from baked mud with a thin veneer of paster on the inside. With one more great heave, I fell backwards as the metal rod came free. I picked it up from the floor and saw the end that had been hidden in the wall was sharp. Thinking as fast as I could, I broke one of the wooden chairs next to where Anna was sitting and freeing a chair leg, I used it as a support block under the plastic tie holding Anna's wrists together. I chopped at the plastic furiously until it broke, freeing her hands. "Just keep sitting there and don't move," I said as I noticed the blood from the incisions was still dripping.

BANG!

Another flash-bang grenade exploded, but I thought it seemed further away than the first.

I speed dialled Pat. "Wait up. I'm going to try and light a fire to guide you in." I had earlier seen a box of matches and firelighters by the fireplace in the torture room. Pulling off my jacket, I rolled it up, threw it into the fireplace, lit a match and set fire to the coat and some firelighters. "Can you see the smoke yet?"

"Sure can. I'll zero in now. See you soon."

"Hang on in there, Anna, the cavalry's here," I said.

CHAPTER TWENTY-SEVEN

DON'T MESS WITH DEAL

I didn't have to wait long. There was a loud clatter as something metal dropped down the chimney, bounced off the fire grate, and landed noisily on the red floor tiles. I shouted up, "Got it, thanks. Drop another one," as I checked the magazine of the Uzi Submachine Gun with its ten-inch barrel. I thought, *Good time to try one of these babies — six-hundred rounds per minute with this 9 millimetre Parabellum version. Don't mess with Deal!*

The second Uzi landed almost precisely on the same tile as the first. Handing the first one to Anna, I said, "Stay put. Use this if you have to. Here's the safety," indicating the Fire, Safety, Automatic selector switch. *Got to get her to a hospital soon,* I thought as I looked closely at the cuts on Anna's neck. "I'll be back soon," I said, trying the door handle. It was locked, but a short burst of automatic fire from my Uzi solved that problem.

I crept out of the torture room, making sure no one was outside before making my way to the front door. Turning the handle slowly, I was relieved to find it wasn't locked. I carefully stuck my head out to scope what was outside. I couldn't see any sicarios, the evil twins, nor was there any sign of El Loco, O'Rourke or Russo. *They must still be at the hacienda*, I thought. A rattle of automatic gunfire startled me. Sensing it came from the adobe rooftops, I ran to shelter behind one of the sicarios' SUVs parked outside the adobe houses. On looking inside the SUV, I saw the key in the ignition. *Careless*, I thought. Crouching down, I also had a good view of the rooftops.

Pat and Jamie were hopping along the adobe flat roofs from one to the next, firing at targets I couldn't see at first. I crawled to a nearby wall on the far side of the narrow street. Clutching the Uzi in my injured hand, I used the uninjured one to vault the four-feet high wall and hide. Another burst of fire prompted me to peer over the wall at the source of the gunfire. I saw Pat firing at several sicarios with Jamie right behind him. It was then I noticed another sicario sneaking up behind Jamie. Before I could fire, Jamie spun and laid down a short burst of automatic fire, dropping the Mexican.

I decided to climb into the SUV and fired up the engine, gunning the motor until I was now level with Pat and Jamie. Opening the window, I hollered, "Pat, Jamie, drop down to me. Jump on to the car roof."

Two loud crashes above my head told me they had followed instructions. Pat jumped into the seat next to me with Jamie flinging herself into the rear seats. "Still got your bag," Pat said, panting for breath.

"Good to meet you, Matt. Pat speaks highly of you." Jamie grinned.

What the fuck? She is a cool customer, I thought.

"Hang on tight," I said as I drove away.

GONE!

"Where are we going?" Pat asked.

"See what lies between us and the hacienda," I said. "I need to get the lie of the land and Anna to a hospital before she bleeds out."

"Man, don't be too long. You need to get Anna out of that adobe place first."

"I know that. You got a timer on your cell?"

"Yeah," Pat said.

"Set it for five minutes," I said.

"Look, why don't I wait with Anna," Jamie said.

"Good idea. Matt?" Pat said.

"Okay, thanks. You want to run back there?" I said after a moment's thought.

I wanted to know if she was up to the task, but as soon as I spoke, Jamie was out of the door as fast as a Japanese bullet train, taking one of the Uzis with her and saying, "Be careful, you two."

I watched in the rear-view mirror as she ate up the yards like an Olympic sprinter. "Where's your wheels?" I said.

"Behind the adobe houses, there's a field. I left it there at the end of a dirt track, along with four dead Mexican cops," Pat said, adding, "She's something else."

"Who?"

"Jamie. She killed one of the cops. Man! You should have seen her," Pat said, almost gleefully.

"Good to hear seeing I've trusted her to look after Anna," I said then out of curiosity, I said, "Green and gold cop car?"

"Yeah, how did you know?"

"Just a guess. We probably bumped into them on the way here when we stopped at a cantina to switch vehicles. Anyway, it's good to know you have wheels in case we need a backup escape plan."

I drove in silence for the next two minutes until I saw the hacienda looming in the near distance. I had taken in everything I needed to know, noting outhouses and horse stables on the route in case we needed to hide somewhere. Now satisfied, I turned to Pat. "Okay, let's get back to Anna and Jamie. How's that timer?"

"Good, only three minutes since I set it," Pat said.

We drove up to the adobe house where Anna and I had been held. There was no sign of activity.

"I don't like this," Pat said. "That's Jamie's forage cap in the dirt, look."

"She could have dropped it," I said.

"Possibly, but I don't buy that she just dropped it."

Parking the stolen SUV outside, I said, "Let's go see."

There was no sign of Anna or Jamie. They had gone.

"Shit!" I yelled. "Think, man, we were away for three minutes."

"The roof. Let's get on the roof. We might see something," Pat said, fishing for the binoculars in my weaponry bag.

Using the SUV's roof first, Pat made it with ease onto the flat roof. He gave me a helping hand on noticing my swollen thumb and finger. "There," Pat shouted, "see the dust. That must be them, and it looks like they're heading for the hacienda," he added as he lowered the binoculars.

"Must be another road then otherwise they would have passed us," I said.

"Yeah, it's a circuit. You can use either way between the hacienda and here," Pat said, continuing to watch. "Wait, yes, Anna and Jamie. They're okay but being taken into the hacienda at gunpoint. Here, take a look."

I took the glasses from Pat and confirmed what he had just said. "Hold up, four sicarios went in with them, and two have just come out. They are standing guard outside the hacienda. Pat, say no if you want. I have an idea."

"Shoot!"

"Take the SUV and act as a decoy. Get those two goons outside the hacienda to chase you."

"What will you do?"

Tapping the Uzi by his side, I said, "Cause some mayhem and get those women out of there."

"But your hand."

"It's nothing. I can't feel any pain. Now, listen, this is the plan in full. Do exactly as I say, and we will all fight another day. Drop me off close to the hacienda and make sure the sicarios outside chase you. I'll explain the rest on the way."

Having switched places, Pat drove and listened carefully. All our lives partly depended on the rangy blond former special forces soldier.

CRAZY RIDE

Pat got as close as he dared to the hacienda so I could make my way on foot to the two-storey white ranch house. Clutching the Uzi, I hid under a bush. Two live grenades and some flash-bangs were hidden inside a small backpack I now wore back to front so I could quickly reach inside for the grenades.

Satisfied Matt was out of sight, Pat fired at the two sicarios standing guard at the front door of the hacienda. One went down, clutching his leg, while the other ran for the red van parked outside the front door. Three more sicarios emerged on to the front porch, offering themselves as targets. Pat fired on fully automatic, and he could hear Matt laying down automatic fire too. Three sicarios dropped now. *How many more inside*, Pat wondered.

The red van's motor could be heard revving hard. The escaped sicario was now pumping away on the horn, bringing three more killers running. Once they were in the van, it set off in Pat's direction. *So good, so far*, thought Pat. *Stand by for a crazy ride, you suckers.*

True to Matt's plan, the van chased Pat in the SUV. He knew where he was heading for, but the cartel killers hadn't got a clue. Pat thrashed the hell out of the stolen sicario's SUV's engine, burning rubber at each curve in the road. On the straight, he outpaced the van so deliberately slowed down a tad. He needed them to follow. *Come to daddy*, he thought. An occasional burst of semi-automatic gunfire from his pursuers never failed to grab his attention. *Two can play at that*, he thought as he held his Uzi one-handed out of the window, spraying the road and van behind him. It seemed like he had been driving for only a few minutes when he saw the Monterrey City sign. Ignoring any speed limits, he continued driving like crazy, whooping and hollering in an adrenaline-fuelled escapade. *I should see it soon*, Pat thought.

I stayed low, still hidden by the bushes but often carefully looking at what was happening at the front of the hacienda. There was nothing. It was quiet. The shot sicarios hadn't stirred, so I guessed between Pat and me, we had killed them. Pulling out Anna's cell phone from the backpack, I speed dialled Elaine Steele. "Thank God, you answered."

"What the hell is happening?" she asked.

"They have Anna and Jamie in El Loco's hacienda. I need backup urgently. Anna's bleeding out, and if I don't get to her soon, she'll die for sure."

"Matt, I already spoke with Colonel Diaz. He's one I can trust, and he's OIC of an elite army task force. I will let him know where you are."

"Thanks, Ellie. Another thing, tell the consulate in Monterrey to let Pat in. He's driving a black SUV stolen from El Loco."

"You got it… and bring Anna home safe and sound."

"I will, I promise."

Pat couldn't miss Old Glory fluttering in the breeze above the American Consulate. He saw it from two miles back. He'd stopped firing at the chasing red van, fearful of hitting innocent people, but that didn't stop them firing at him. He did a ninety-degree turn into the long cement road leading to the consulate, almost on two wheels at one point. The red van was close behind him, too close. He could see the security gate and booth at the entrance and knew he could not afford the niceties of producing identification to the U.S. Marine guards unless he wanted to end up dead. *Only one thing for it*, he thought. Stepping on the gas pedal for all he was worth, he ignored the signals to halt and the warning shots and crashed straight through the barrier. *I hope they knew I was expected*, he grinned to himself.

Whipping the steering wheel around violently, he did a complete handbrake turn so he was now facing out towards the pursuing van. The sicarios continued firing with semi-automatics, which was their mistake. A volley of shots rang out as the Marine Security Guard personnel realised what was happening. Pat didn't hesitate in laying down automatic fire from the Uzi. The red van's windshield disappeared in shards of glass as the front seat occupants slumped back in their seats, bloodied and mortally wounded. Still Pat and the Marines laid down fire until the van exploded moments after Pat had burst through the barrier.

The security booth was still intact, so two of the Marines ushered Pat at gunpoint to a telephone extension in the booth. The young Marine in the booth said, "This had better be good. Here, there's a call patched through from Special Agent Steele," as he handed over the phone.

"Elaine?"

"Yes, Pat, are you okay?"

"A bit out of breath and pumped up, but apart from that, I'm fine."

"Good, has a Mexican colonel arrived yet… Colonel Diaz?"

"No… wait up… maybe… I hear a chopper… wait… yeah… Mexican markings. I guess it's him."

"He's in charge of the rescue. Just do as he says and get them back in one piece, will you?"

"I will, thanks. What do I tell the Marines here?"

"Put them on the phone to me," Steele said. Pat immediately handed it to the serious-faced young Marine.

Pat saw the chopper land in the compound next to the main building. A big guy dressed in a leather jacket beckoned him over. Unimpeded by Marines or anyone else, Pat ran the fifty yards, stooping as the downdraft got stronger. The big guy held out his hand to help Pat inside the chopper as quickly as possible as the pilot got the machine up and off the ground within seconds. The big leather-jacketed guy handed him an intercom headset, and once Pat had fixed it to his head, he heard, "I'm Colonel Miguel Diaz, Mike to my American friends. We are going to have some fun, yes?"

"Not so sure I'd describe it as fun. This is El Loco we are dealing with," Pat said.

Diaz laughed heartily, gesturing to the firepower on board the chopper. "Even El Loco is not immune to my cannon here."

Pat looks all around him, surveying the firepower with expert eyes, before saying, "Man! Cannon, machine gun and a rocket launcher. Cool!"

"Do not worry, *güero*, we will rescue your friends and then kill El Loco. I have been waiting for this for a long time."

CHAPTER THIRTY

THE ZONE

Switching the backpack to the conventional position, I started crawling towards the hacienda porch. Holding the Uzi ready in my left hand, I ignored the pain in my right. I was in the zone, blocking out all sensation of pain from my hand and ribs, a technique I learned from my martial arts training in Asia. I recited this in my head as it aided me in blocking the pain. Standing slowly, I surveyed the porch, checking for any signs of movement. Satisfied all the prone sicarios lying on the veranda were dead, I padded up to the open front door, a vast hardwood affair decorated Mexican style. Taking a furtive look inside, I saw a large living room filled with furniture with a sizeable fireplace to the rear. Satisfied the space was empty of people, I switched the backpack again, removing a flash-bang, so named because on detonating it emits a bright light and ear-piercing explosive sound intended to debilitate and disorientate all who are near it. Once the pin was pulled, and a count to three, I lobbed it towards the fireplace. It landed with a clatter on the hardwood floor. Before the detonation, I saw a man run from a dark alcove then stoop to collect the grenade. *Another sicario*, I thought as I ducked outside again.

The sicario threw the grenade through the open door, no doubt relieved to hear it explode harmlessly beyond the porch. From cover behind the door, I lay down a short burst from the Uzi, then removing another grenade from the backpack threw it inside after removing the pin. Another burst of fire from me ensured the hired killer stayed hidden inside the living room. *See if you like this, amigo*, I thought as the live grenade shattered into small sharp shrapnel fragments followed by an unholy scream. *It's time for me to introduce myself*, I thought as I entered the room with Uzi ready.

With a roar, the Mexican killer upturned a sofa he had been sheltering behind, now torn to shreds by grenade shrapnel, and rushed me once I had taken a few steps inside the room. It was enough to surprise me. I was too slow in raising my Uzi but not too slow to release the backpack, leaving me free to fight unencumbered. *Here we go again*, I thought, *just like slo-mo in a movie when it's a fight to the death.*

At that thought, I saw the sicario had only one arm. The left arm was a bloody stump with bloodstained shirt material hanging from it. *Wounded animal*, I thought. Again a fraction too late to react, I was winded as the sicario barged me to the floor, forcing me to lose my grip on the Uzi. The Mexican lay on top of me holding a long blade in his right hand, which he thrust towards my throat. Using all the strength in my leg muscles, I kicked and rolled over at the same time, forcing the sicario sideways and making him land onto his bloody stump. As the Mexican released the knife, howling in agony, I got to my feet and kicked him several times in the face until he stopped moving. Retrieving my Uzi, I put one round in between the sicario's eyes. He was going to die anyway. I just sped up the process.

Silence, so figuring there were no more hired killers nearby, I yelled, "Anna! Anna! Jamie!" Again silence. *No*, I thought, *I will find you.*

Still there was silence after I called out three more times.

Following my third shout of, "Anna!" each one louder than the last, I heard, "Deal, come and join us and your friends. You really must see this for yourself." I recognised the voice. It was O'Rourke's. "Come on, join the party before we chopper out of here," he mocked.

I then heard the distant blade slap of an approaching helicopter. *Fuck no, they mustn't escape.*

CHAPTER THIRTY-ONE

CROCODILE

I followed the direction of O'Rourke's derisive invitation to a courtyard within a quadrangle set in the middle of the hacienda complex. Unable to see anyone, I called out, "Where are you? Let me see Anna."

"Walk through the archway, Chucky," El Loco said. "You can see what I've done to your *puta,* just like my men did to your whore ex-wife in Miami."

El Loco, O'Rourke, probably Russo, who else? I thought.

Uzi in hand, I strode through the arch topped with a bougainvillea fresco where I stopped in my tracks, frozen at what I saw.

"Put down the gun, Deal," El Loco ordered. "One word from me and your bitch will be lowered into the water." As he spoke, he tore off some meat from a rack of pork ribs then threw it into the pool. The water exploded with a thrash of a crocodile's tail. "My pet Nile crocodile is hungry, see," he said, laughing.

Anna was tied to a bar spanning the pool and hanging upside down over the pool with one of El Loco's men standing by a winch handle ready to lower her closer to the pool. It looked like they had made some fresh cuts to her neck with blood dripping into the water and she was also gagged with duct tape across her mouth.

"I see I have no choice," I said. "Get her down, and I will throw down my gun."

O'Rourke laughed. "Your whore stays there until she either bleeds out or the crocodile has her for supper. So, throw down your fucking gun, asswipe."

I placed the Uzi on the tiled floor, then the backpack. "Okay. What next? And where's Jamie?"

"I'm here, Matt," Jamie called out. I looked over beyond the cartel leader, Russo and O'Rourke. Jamie was trussed like a Christmas turkey with her legs bound to her arms.

"You okay," I said.

"Apart from pins and needles, yes," she said.

"Good girl, I'll get you both out of here if it's the last thing I do. I promise," but I knew that was part bravado. *Think, man.*

"Cut the crap, Deal," Russo said. "No one's going nowhere. You're all dead meat, one way or another," he snarled.

I slowly approached the table separating me from my enemies. It was laden with Lechon, ribs, and carafes of red wine. As I did the slow walk, I felt for the backup revolver tucked in a hidden pocket stitched into my pants' waistband. Deftly, as a result of much practice, I emptied the gun's chamber of all six bullets before quietly snapping the chamber back in place. Sighing, I said, "You know what?" in an exhausted voice.

"What? Enlighten us, amuse us even," O'Rourke said.

"O'Rourke, have you got other kids?"

"Two, why?"

"Here's the thing. I killed one. You have two others. If I kill you, they will probably come after me. I'm weary. Tired of all this shit. Same with you, Russo. I kill you, some other gangster is coming for me. I can't live like that anymore."

"All very touching. What are we supposed to do, let you all go, and you promise not to kill us? Deal, you are a prize asshole. We have guns. You have fuck all," O'Rourke said.

Feeling in my waistband, I grasped the butt of the hidden .38 snub-nose revolver. With one swift movement, I aimed at O'Rourke's head. "Let me prove it. I can kill you right now before Russo or your Mexican friend can bat an eyelid, but I won't. I'll spare you your life for mine and the women. Here, have it." I set the gun down on the table in front of O'Rourke and turned around.

Taking a few steps away from the table, I heard the revolver hammer – *click, click.* Not waiting for another click, I spun around lightly on my heels, and by the time of the third click, was holding O'Rourke by his lapels, dragging him over the table. I pull O'Rourke over to the nearest wall a few steps away, turning him so we both faced the wall, and smashed his face into a metal wall light fitting set at a right angle to the floor. O'Rourke's nose and face exploded into a blur of blood and snot, but I wasn't yet finished. With both hands, I pulled back on O'Rourke's head, then propelled it forward into the damaged and broken metal light fitting shaft. The exposed metal penetrated the American's eye before piercing the eye socket, then the brain. I pulled him away, and he dropped down stone dead at my feet.

"Drop those guns," an unfamiliar loud voice boomed.

El Loco and Russo had guns pointing at me. Still, I can only guess they were too fascinated or overawed by the speed, audacity and sheer violence of O'Rourke's execution to intervene. They like killing, you see. They can stand by and admire a killer at work. A killer like me. The difference between them and me is I don't like killing, but I will if my loved ones or I am in danger. That fascination of theirs probably saved my life.

"Drop those guns," I heard once more, but this time there was even more urgency in the demand. Together with El Loco and Russo, I turned to see who had spoken. We all wheeled about towards the voice to see a big Mexican guy I later got to know as Colonel Diaz, Pat, and four Mexican Task Force uniformed soldiers. "Now!" Diaz spoke once more.

The cartel leader, *jefe*, his sicario winchman, Russo, *capo,* and his two New Jersey Mob wise guys complied, holding up their hands in surrender.

"Quick, get Anna down off there," I shouted.

Diaz snapped off some orders in Spanish, which sent his men running off. They returned a few minutes later carrying extendable ladders and some left-over sheets of boarding. They were smart and well-trained, taking no time at all to lay the ladder with the boarding laid on top to act as a bridge across the pool. I was impressed but had one question. "What about the crocodile?"

Diaz didn't bother to answer but instead walked over to El Loco, dragged him screaming for his life to the pool edge and pushed the crazy cartel leader into the water. "Two problems solved," he said quietly under his breath. "That's my revenge, and the crocodile is fed."

The soldiers untied Anna, removed the gag, and gently lowered her onto the makeshift bridge before carrying her to the table which I had cleared of food, drinks and everything else. "We have a medic," Diaz said. "Let him check her out."

I held Anna's head and kissed her on the forehead. "We are going home," I whispered. She squeezed my hand weakly.

Through dry lips, she said almost inaudibly, "I knew you'd come. Take me home, please."

I could not cry even though I wanted to. I did hear that deep intake of breath in my chest rise and stop in my throat that sometimes happens when something deeply emotional makes you shudder.

CHAPTER THIRTY-TWO

AN UNDERSTANDING

The medic checked out both women, declaring Anna fit to be moved to hospital and Jamie unharmed, apart from some bruises to her face sustained when she fought back after the sicarios captured her and Anna at the adobe house.

Colonel Diaz retook charge, arranging for Anna to be flown by helicopter to the prestigious Sisters of Mercy Hospital in Monterrey. "We wait here for the chopper to return," he instructed.

"I'm going with her," I protested as I brushed aside the colonel to get to the chopper.

"There's no room. Besides, I need to talk to you in private. Pat, you go with the two women. Matt will join you later, and he can get his injuries attended to then."

I knew Diaz was serious. Reluctantly, I agreed, and I was also struck by the man's natural air of authority – a man you didn't argue with unless you wanted to end up with a crocodile in a swimming pool. What was more important, he made me feel safe, and if I thought that way I knew Anna was in good hands.

"Okay, I guess you know what you're doing," I said.

Diaz ignored me and continued to organise his men to ferry Anna on an improvised gurney. Jamie, bruised and battered, managed the walk to the chopper with Pat leading her. The machine had landed earlier on the far side of the courtyard outside the hacienda. I realised then it was the helicopter I had heard earlier and not the one Russo and O'Rourke were expecting.

I watched with sadness with only Diaz and the remainder of his men as company as the chopper took off. It hovered for a short while before flying off in the direction of Monterrey city and the hospital.

Diaz beckoned me inside, leaving his soldiers on the porch. "Time for our talk, my friend," Diaz said.

Ignoring the scene of death and mayhem in the living room, we sat down close together in two sumptuous armchairs. "What is it you have to say?" I asked.

"First, the good. You and Pat did a great job here, Jamie too from what I gather. That's no surprise because Ellie told me all about you."

"Ellie? You must be a close friend of hers?"

"We are. We met at Quantico just before her transfer to Florida. I hear you two worked together before her secondment from London," Diaz said. "She's a fine woman and a great cop. How come you're not a detective anymore?"

"She's not told you?" I said.

"No, the call I got from her about you guys is one of the few times I've spoken with her since she left Virginia and transferred to Florida. She only told me what I needed to know and said it was an urgent matter of life or death. That was all, so I got my shit together, assembled a small tactical team and choppered into the consulate where I met Pat."

"Your English has no trace of Mexican," I said in curiosity.

"I'm Tex-Mex, a Tejano, born here in this province of Mexican parents but raised in Texas, so I have dual nationality. I moved back after my mom and pop died."

"Then you joined the Mexican Army?" I said.

"I did."

"Why?"

"I figured it was the least corrupt outfit I could join in fighting the drug cartels."

"Wait up, this has something to do with the deaths of your parents, right?"

"Damn right! It was El Loco's men who killed them because they refused to smuggle cash into Mexico, the proceeds of selling drugs. I have been waiting for this day for a long time and thanks to you, I have avenged my parents' murders."

"Now, I understand you, Colonel," I said.

"Mike, call me Mike. Now, I asked you a question before we veered off somewhere else."

"Remind me," I said.

"I asked you why you are no longer a detective."

"Easy one but a long story."

"We got time, and I want to know all about Ellie's friends. You obviously mean a lot to her."

"For one, I thought I… and Anna, were the only people who know her as Ellie. Two, we worked together as detectives on the new NCA, National Crime Agency, in England and before that on the Human Trafficking Squad. Three, I killed a guy in

England and was charged with murder, so with the help of Anna and Ellie, I skipped the country and came back to live in Florida. That's when this trouble started."

"That much, I do know. Ellie told me about your daughter Mercy and how you hunted down the scum behind the attack on her," Diaz said, "but you still haven't really answered my question."

"I got cleared of the murder rap, but I had no inclination to return to London or my old job, so I started a P.I. business in Florida which means technically I'm still a detective," I said to convince myself I was still a detective.

"If you say so. Listen here, this is the bad news."

"Go on," I said.

"I can't have you repeating anything like this in Mexico, do you hear me?"

"You got my solemn promise."

"I'm fucking serious," Diaz said, noting the slight smile on my face.

"Hell! So am I. I might just run for sheriff or something back in Florida, go fishing or raise my kid," I said, raising my voice.

"Mercy? I thought she was still in a coma with not much chance of pulling through," Diaz said as if treading on thin ice.

"No, Anna's pregnant."

"That's great news," Diaz said. "It will soften the blow," he added.

"What the fuck are you saying?"

"Don't get mad at me. I promised Ellie she would be the one to break the news, but now I feel I must tell you," Diaz said wistfully.

"Stop talking in riddles, please."

"Matt, Mercy died yesterday."

CHAPTER THIRTY-THREE

DARK HUMOUR

"My condolences," Diaz said. "I'll leave you in peace while I make some arrangements to take the Americans into custody."

"Thanks, where are they going?" I asked.

"Not sure yet. Local jails are not a good idea. They might bribe their way free. I'm going to call Ellie to see if we can hand them over at the border."

"What happened to El Loco's guy, the one operating the winch?"

"My friend, some questions are better not asked, but if you really must know I told him to move and make it snappy so with that, he threw himself into the pool with the croc," Diaz said with a straight face.

I looked up to see the slow smile spreading across Diaz's mouth and couldn't help myself in saying, "See you later, alligator."

"In a while, crocodile," Diaz said before leaving me alone with my thoughts.

As I watched him stride purposefully away, I thought, *Cop and soldiers' humour is the same – the black kind.* Grateful to Diaz in that I had been distracted for a while thinking of the loss of Mercy, I felt a little odd – relieved that she was now at peace and not relying on machines to keep her alive. *Alive!* I thought. *What a joke,* as I vividly recalled the day she skipped out of the front door. I saw my fresh, beautiful daughter before she was grossly violated in every conceivable way at the hands of Conor O'Rourke and his frat rapist friends. I paused and looked to heaven with tears in my eyes and silently prayed: *Mercy if I have done wrong, then it was for you. I killed O'Rourke and his son to avenge you. Lord, forgive me and send me a message.*

Diaz returned, having decided to use another detachment of his men to escort Russo and his two men to Laredo by transport helicopter where they would perform a handover at the border to the U.S. Marshals. Elaine Steele had drawn up a holding indictment naming all three men in the kidnapping of Anna and me.

The colonel then arranged for me to join up with Anna who had earlier been flown to Monterrey's Sisters of Mercy hospital in the gunship helicopter, courtesy of Colonel Mike Diaz and the Mexican Army. It struck me as ironic that Anna was being treated in a hospital bearing the name of my late, beloved daughter. On the short flight, I pulled out a photograph of Mercy from my wallet, taken shortly before the night she was brutally assaulted on the Destin beach. As I traced my finger over her strawberry blonde hair and then to her pink lips, I broke down and cried. I think Mike Diaz and the other soldiers on board deliberately averted their collective gaze to give me some privacy and to let me grieve.

I could not hear the rotors. All noise was suddenly blocked out by the sweetest singing noise but like the voice of an angel. "Daddy, please don't be sad. I'm fine, and I'm safe now. I know you will take care of your new baby girl and Anna will be the best mommy. I love you."

The startled crew, including Diaz, stared at me as I loudly exclaimed, "Did you hear that?" All I got by way of any kind of acknowledgement was a collective perfunctory head shake.

CHAPTER THIRTY-FOUR

KEEP IT

Colonel Mike Diaz was turning out to be a great friend and a useful asset. He made no fuss about returning my bag of weapons to me, including the Uzis used by Pat, Jamie and me. Diaz had even managed to retrieve the Uzi taken from Anna when she and Jamie were abducted at the adobe house to the hacienda. On handing me the bag before we left Mexico, he said, "Nice piece," as he examined one of the Uzis in the bag.

I had no hesitation as I said, "Keep it." I knew he would put it to good use.

Three days later, Mike Diaz flew with me, Anna, Pat and Jamie in a small twin-engine plane, landing at a deserted airfield in Texas where we were met by an excited Special Agent Elaine Steele.

"I see you have commandeered another army asset, Mike," Steele said before embracing him. Diaz was first off the plane, followed by Anna. "Well, look at you. A few more days R&R and you'll be ready for anything," Steele said, breaking off from Diaz.

Anna lightly fingered the dressings on her neck, smiled and said, "Maybe. It's simply good to be back. No offence to you or Mexico, Mike."

"None taken," Diaz said. "Talking about R&R, I have a week off, so I hope you're going to show me the bright lights of Destin."

"All arranged, Mike, though I wouldn't say they are bright lights, exactly," Steele said as she glanced across at the aircraft.

Hopping off the plane onto the tarmac, I saw Ellie running towards me. She wrapped her arms tightly about me before saying, "Matt, I am so, so sorry about Mercy. I was going to tell you first, but I understand Mike felt the time was right to tell you."

"Thanks, Ellie. She's at peace, and so am I. And thanks for all you did, especially getting hold of this big guy," I said nodding in the direction of Diaz.

"We'll second that, won't we Jamie?" Pat piped up as he led Jamie by the hand down the aircraft steps.

"You bet," Jamie said. "He can fix everything, except my Aunt Bessie's pickup truck is still in Monterrey."

Diaz said, "If that's what you think, you'd better think again, young woman."

"What do you mean?" Jamie inquired.

"Look over there… in the parking lot." Diaz pointed behind her. "I arranged for one of my men to find it which he did, as you can see. Not only that, he drove it here."

"This is beyond words, so I'll give you a great big hug instead," Jamie said, "and please thank the driver."

"Go thank him yourself. He's right there. On second thoughts, I'll wave him over as he's going back on this plane," Diaz said, waving to his man.

"You're quiet, Pat, all okay?" Steele said.

"Fine. A tad disappointed though," he said.

"How come?" Steele said.

"I never got to fire the cannon or the rocket launcher on that chopper," Pat said laughing.

"Ha! Just as well. From what I hear, last time you fired a rocket it caused mayhem," Diaz said, patting Pat on the back with his huge hand. "Down Tallahassee way if I'm not mistaken."

"The less I hear about that day, the better. I'm done with mayhem, done with killing. Anna let's go home," I said, taking her by the hand.

"Right, well said, Matt. Mike, Anna, Matt, follow me to my jet over there. Well, not mine exactly… let's say borrowed from the United States Government," Steele said. "Pat, I'm assuming you and Jamie are taking the truck back to Aunt Bessie?"

"We are, then I'll get my car and drive on up to Destin with Jamie, if that's okay with you guys?"

"Fine with us, isn't it, Matt?" Anna said. Looking at my expression, she asked, "What's the frown for?"

"Nothing," I said. "Let's go."

The government Lear jet took off from the Texas airstrip with Pat and Jamie waving farewell, and it covered the eight hundred miles or so in just under two hours, landing at the Pensacola Naval Air Base having received a special government clearance. The flight was undertaken in almost total silence with

Anna and I content to relax to forget our recent ordeal. The silence was only broken with Steele confirming accommodation arrangements, as she felt it best for Anna and me to stay elsewhere in Destin other than our top floor apartment at Matt's Big Deal Gym or our secret bunker. In any event, she knew a key staff member was dead with the murder of Bobby Peters.

Steele rightly reckoned her friends needed to fix that issue once they felt ready to pick up the pieces. We didn't require convincing, so Anna and I accepted the arrangements for us to stay in a privately rented house on the beachfront at Navarre Beach, close to where I used to live with Lorey when Mercy was still alive. Of course, Elaine checked this with both of us. It was a great idea, and we welcomed the chance to relax at the house with a balcony deck overlooking the warm waters of the Gulf of Mexico.

Before disembarking, Steele chose the right moment to mention a funeral. "Matt, I hope you don't mind, but I've arranged for Mercy's funeral. And that of Bobby Peters, is that okay?"

"No, I don't mind one bit. When?"

"Mercy is two days from now, Wednesday. St. Mary's Cemetery in Fort Walton. Bobby's is the day after at Destin Memorial Cemetery."

"Okay, get them to send me the tab, will you?"

"We can sort that out later," Ellie said.

"Thanks, you are a real friend," I said, unbuckling my safety belt, as I stood up and leaned over to her in the opposite seat to me and kissed her on the cheek.

"So are you, Matt, and you… my sister Anna," Steele said.

"You two sisters?" Diaz said, not wishing to interrupt but curious as they looked nothing like each other.

Anna and Ellie laughed. "Mike, you don't forget much, but I told you when we first met. Anna, will you tell him or me?" Ellie said.

"We are but not as you know it. We are sisters in spirit. It goes back a while now," Anna said.

Diaz looked confused and said nothing.

It was only at that point I remembered my car was still in Galveston. "Hey, Ellie. What with all the excitement, I clean forgot my car is still parked at the resort in Galveston."

"One step ahead of you, Matt, as usual. I checked with Galveston P.D. It was stolen and burnt out when the thieves dumped it. Hope you're insured."

"I am. They have done me a favour seeing it was eight years' old."

Smiling, I looked across to Mike Diaz, who seemed to be still figuring out the 'sister thing.' I smiled some more.

CHAPTER THIRTY-FIVE

AT REST

Mercy's funeral was the quiet affair you would expect with only one living relative left on this Earth – me, her father. Her mother, Lorey Hughes, once Deal although she never used that name, and who eventually became Braithwaite, was dead. Jack Hughes, Mercy's grandfather, was also dead, not that he would have been welcome seeing he was involved in the bribing of Captain Stevenson, the chief of detectives, to lose the evidence which would have condemned Mercy's rapists to lengthy jail sentences.

The priest was a pleasant young man, Anna and I agreed upon that. Pat, Jamie, Mike Diaz, Sandy Grant and of course Elaine Steele were all present to pay their last respects. Anna and I had a quiet conversation about Mike and Ellie in the car on the way back to the gym. "You think something is going on there?" I said.

"Of course there is. They look perfect together, don't you think, or have you still got a thing for your old flame?"

"Get out of here!" I said, smiling. "I'm an old married man."

"Married? To whom, may I ask?"

"No one, not yet, but I'm tired of funerals. Let's get married," I said.

Anna leaned over from the front passenger seat to kiss me. "Mwaahhh! I love you, Matt Deal. Yes, let's do it."

"Hey! I'm driving," I said, "and on a more serious note… far more serious than marriage, what do you say about Pat and Jamie running the gym, at least temporarily?"

"I think it's an excellent idea. Jamie's already well-liked in the gym. With a bit of training, she could end up being a martial arts instructor."

"Those are my thoughts, too. I wonder where she learned to fight like that?" I said.

"We will have to ask them, of course, but what about the P.I. side of things?" Anna asked.

"Think I'll drop it. Mike was asking me about the detective thing back in Mexico. I told him I might go for being a sheriff."

"Wow! Really? You'd look good in uniform. Promise me you'll wear it when you come to bed." Anna winked as she said it.

"Only if you wear a nurse's uniform." I smiled.

"You know what, Matt Deal?"

"What?"

"You are a dirty old man. Now, get me home to our bed."

"I'll tell you something, now, Anna-soon-to-be-Deal, I don't feel bad at all about talking like this right after Mercy's funeral. I know it's what she would want... for us to be happy. You know, I swore she spoke to me back in the chopper in Mexico on the way to the hospital to see you. She mentioned our baby girl, and we don't know if it's a girl or a boy."

"Girl? I guess it may have been Mercy sending a message to you. That's very good. It could have been her. You know, I'm not one who scoffs at such stuff. Just because she's passed doesn't mean we ever forget her," Anna said with a tear forming in her eye.

"Another thing... I'm kinda relieved she's no longer lying in that hospital kept alive by machines," I said.

"Come on, let's go home, Sheriff."

The following day it was the turn of Bobby Peters to be interred at his final resting place. Once more, the same mourners attended. Anna and I, Pat, Jamie, Elaine Steele, Sandy Grant and Mike Diaz, who was on his last day of R & R before returning to Mexico, were all present. Bobby's grandmother had been cremated earlier the same day with only Sandy Grant attending the chapel within the Destin Memorial Gardens.

CHRISTMAS

Three weeks later

We loved the rented beach house so much we inquired if we could take it on a longer lease and celebrated when the owner agreed to a two-year-long rental. It was a perfect place to unwind after the Mexican ordeal and was a great help to Anna, who was getting used to not only her first pregnancy but also the idea of becoming a mother.

The two-storey clapboard house built on stilts was right next to the coastal highway on Navarre Beach, a short walk away from the brilliant white sands. It had a wooden second-floor deck built around the house which afforded a patio area with a view to the ocean. I say the second floor as the first was the empty area underneath from where the thick wooden piles were set that supported the whole building. I think that style is a Florida hurricane thing as the piles are placed into a fair few feet of concrete to act as an anchor in extreme weather conditions. That second floor comprised of a living room, kitchen and the main bedroom which had a self-contained bathroom. On top of that floor, there were two spare bedrooms and another bathroom.

Outside, there was a front and back yard. The front was mostly cemented over for parking space, but the back yard was complete with a volleyball net and a metal stake in the sandy soil for playing horseshoes, a game I enjoyed.

I also sorted out a replacement for the old burnt-out SUV. I'd had that since I opened the gym and before I went to England. I didn't tell Anna, but I was glad to see it disappear as it was a parting gift from my then father-in-law Jack Hughes as part of the bribe to persuade me to go to England after Mercy had been attacked. The rest of his 'persuasion' was a veiled threat when he showed me photos of his Mob connections—those connections which had now been laid bare.

It was with a feeling of rebirth and joy when I took the keys of a new Chevrolet Trailblazer on lease. I figured the insurance payout for the old car would make a handsome down payment so impetuously I dipped into my savings to fund the initial cost, praying the insurance cheque would soon arrive. I had also arranged for Anna's Harley to be moved from Bobby's grandma's home to our new beach house. Anna was delighted and took it for frequent short spins up and down the coastal highway saying, "I won't be able to do this soon," as she gestured to exaggerate the size of her belly. Unspoken between us, but I knew Anna was thinking of Sheba and how she would have loved this home.

These were perfect days. This period was a long lull after the storms of Galveston and Mexico, not to mention the shootings at Tallahassee involving so many deaths and the near-fatal shooting of Anna. I was tired of all that and prayed for peaceful days ahead for my new family. This time together allowed us to discuss plans. I had also realised it was Christmas Day the day after we signed the extended lease. With recent events, we hadn't given Christmas a thought.

I toyed with the idea of driving over to my favourite supermarket, Publix on Route 98 where I often shopped, mostly to satisfy Anna's cravings for sushi as they had a superb sushi deli counter, to buy a ready meal for Christmas lunch at home. Then I had a better idea. We both liked the vibe and the food at Juana's, a pagoda-like restaurant right next to the Navarre Causeway so when I mooted the idea, Anna gave it the proverbial thumbs up. We were also in agreement we wouldn't exchange presents but instead open a savings account for our expected new arrival, our baby.

On Christmas Day morning, we talked seriously about the gym business.

"I had a good talk with Jamie. She's keen on the idea but… and there are two buts, really," Anna said over breakfast taken outside on the deck of our new home as we now called it since signing the extended lease.

"Out with it... or them," I said, correcting myself.

"Okay, the easier of the two first. Pat is taking his trucker test. If he passes, he wants to buy a rig, so that means a lot of travelling all over the country, so Jamie's not too sure just yet."

"And the second but?"

"She *is a he*," Anna said, studying my face for a reaction.

"What!"

"She's transgender."

"You keep saying *she* when *she is a he*. I don't get it."

"Because she feels like *she, not he*. I can understand that, and so should you. After all, it's her body, her life. And from what she told me; she's had a terrible life until meeting Pat."

"So, Pat knows?"

"Yeah, of course, he does. They have sex, you know," Anna said, and I could see from her expression she was getting annoyed with me.

I thought about this for a moment, then pointed down between my legs, "Look. Sorry to be crude but does *she… he,* have a dick or a vagina?" I settled for using *vagina,* so I wasn't crude really, but it made no difference.

"Matt! For goodness sake. What difference does it make… to you… or anyone else for that matter? If Pat is okay with it and it makes them both happy… oh, what the fuck, I can't believe you are like this. Now, you sit there while I tell you exactly what a crap life she's had," Anna said, her voice betraying her frustration.

"There you go again… *she's* had," I said. I wanted to back out of this discussion and wished I'd never started it. It was something I was unable to get my head around for some reason and rather than retire gracefully, I knew I'd just added fuel to the fire.

Picking up a slice of toast, Anna threw it at me but didn't say a word. It did the trick as I raised my hands in surrender and said softly, "Okay, okay, sorry. Just shocked is all. Tell me all about *her.*" Anna glowered at me on the emphasis of 'her.'

Hands raised in mock defeat, I shut up while Anna continued, "Do not dare interrupt me, Matt Deal. Okay, Jamie was born James, known to her family as Jimmy until she got to about fourteen. That's when Jamie started feeling uncomfortable about her body. In short, she felt like a young woman, not a young man. She decided to dress, look and act like a woman, and that led to a colossal argument at home when her father beat her black and blue. Her Thai mother understood, but that caused friction between her parents, so much so that the father killed Jamie's mother after an argument over Jamie. This was when Jamie was sixteen, and after that, she ran away to a different town in Texas to go live with her Aunt Bessie, her mother's sister, who was as understanding as Jamie's mother.

"When she got to eighteen, she saved enough money from her waitress job… well, more like a hostess at some sleazy Corpus Christi cabaret joint. You know, the kind of place where they serve cocktails with names like 'Pink Pussy,' and 'Sex on the Beach.'"

"How would I know?" I said ingenuously.

"Shut up and listen… then she joined the army in Thailand. On coming back, she started a series of operations and hormone treatment. She's had buttock and thigh implants and an operation to reduce the size of her Adam's apple. She also had breast implants, not that you'd notice, but she told me she wanted small boobs just like her mother and aunt. So, what you see now is a tall, slim beautiful woman, and that's who Pat fell in love with, whether you like it or not."

"Okay, okay but they can't do it normally, can they?" Matt said.

"What the fuck is normal? If you mean she hasn't got a pussy, then right, they do it another way… but is that abnormal, Matt?"

I smiled before answering. Pussy sounds better than a vagina. "Not for a gay man, I guess. I was right all along about him."

"You are impossible, Matt Deal. Your attitudes are stuck right back in the twentieth century, if not the nineteenth."

"That's what I feel, and I will not apologise for that. Besides, where the fuck did she learn to fight like that, all that unarmed combat stuff."

"The Thai army. Her passport shows male gender, so she 'manned' up a bit and enlisted as she was born in Thailand, so no issues arose there. After two years she left and came back to the States as Jamie again."

"That was some long talk you had with *her*. Let me think about it."

"You do just that, mister, or it'll be more than toast I throw next time. And please, quit that *her* thing," Anna said, imitating my emphasis.

I got the message and later that day our Christmas lunch was a pleasant trip out with a few beers for me and Anna drinking the house speciality fruit-based non-alcoholic cocktails. She drove us home even though it's all of five minutes from Juana's to our place. The last thing we needed right now was me being arrested for DUI.

CHAPTER THIRTY-SEVEN

CELEBRATION

One Week Later, January 2032

"Pat has passed his trucker test so what say you we have a celebration, and we can also announce our special news," Anna said.

"Good idea, what about the place we had our first date," I said.

"The Italian restaurant in Sandestin?"

"That's the one."

"Okay, I'll make a reservation for six then," Anna said.

"Six?"

"Yeah, me, you, Sandy, Pat, Jamie and Ellie."

"Jamie?"

"Don't start again. Yes, Jamie."

Elaine Steele arrived at the Vecchia Roma restaurant first, and after informing the *maître d'* she was part of a party of six, she was shown to the reserved table. A few moments later, the wine waiter took her order for a vodka and tonic and gave her the menu to peruse as well as a wine list. While waiting, she checked her cell for messages and broke into a broad smile on reading the text from Mike Diaz:

CONGRATULATIONS! SEE MORE OF
YOU IN TEXAS

Her thoughts of Mike dissipated on hearing, "Cat got the cream, huh?"

We gave Sandy a ride to the restaurant, and as we walked in, I saw Elaine sitting at what appeared to be our reserved table. She was looking at her cell phone and smiling when I heard Anna say, "Cat got the cream, huh?"

As we settled into our seats, Elaine answered, "Not really. Anyway, it's Pat's celebration. Talking of… here they are now."

Pat had smartened up a little, his long blond hair a tad shorter than usual and tied in a ponytail. But all eyes were on the stunning Jamie. She wore a red satin dress, Chinese-style, with a high collar and long slits at the thigh revealing long, slim, coffee-coloured legs. The colour highlighted her dusky mixed-race skin. Her black hair, cut in her usual urchin style, tapered at the back to accentuate her delicate neck, and her hair shone as did the radiance from her face with the broadest smile giving truth to why Thailand was known as 'The Land of Smiles.'

Anna and Ellie stood, and first hugged Jamie then kissed her on the cheek before they repeated the same with Pat. I was last to stand. I felt uncomfortable, and it showed as Anna later told me. Pat offered me his hand, and I took it congratulating him on his pass. Out of the corner of my eye, I could see Anna squirming as if she were watching for my next move. I took a deep breath and thought, *What the hell. You only live once,* and with that broke into a smile as wide as the Mississippi. "You look gorgeous," I said, taking Jamie by the hand. "Permit me to kiss you," I added in what for me was an unnatural, stiff manner. I placed my arms around

Jamie, softly kissing her on her cheek. "You smell gorgeous too. Pat's a lucky man."

"I sure am," Pat said.

"And I'm a lucky woman," Jamie said.

The pre-ordered champagne arrived as we all took our seats. The wine waiter popped the cork then filled up the flutes for all. "Congratulations to Pat," I said as a toast. "Not only for becoming a trucker but also for capturing the beautiful woman he loves. Here's to Jamie and Pat."

"Jamie and Pat," everyone chorused as I glanced over to Anna, and it was evident from her look she had felt an immense relief wash over her.

The antipasti were enjoyed by all, and before the entrée arrived, Elaine spoke. "I have an announcement too. I'm being transferred to El Paso."

"Texas?" Jamie said.

"The one and only… not sure if it is… but yes, the one in Texas," Elaine said.

"Closer to Mike Diaz, then, Ellie?" Anna said.

"Yes. I just got a text from him congratulating me, and he did mention that," Elaine said.

"I bet he did," I said which caused them all to laugh out loud.

"Matt? Shall I tell them or you?" Anna asked.

"You."

"Well, not wanting to best anyone, but we have two announcements. The first is I have said yes to marrying Matthew Deal. The second is…"

Her words were drowned out by loud hollering and cheering from Sandy, Elaine, Pat and Jamie. "Okay, listen guys… I have had my first scan and…"

"It's a girl!" I yelled.

The mixed shouts of "Wow!" "Congratulations!" from the table were followed by Jamie's simple question. "Have you got a name in mind?"

"We have," Anna said and looked at me.

"Merciful, and yes we know as she gets older her friends will call her Merci, but that's cool," I said. "And before anyone asks, we do feel merciful for many things… Anna surviving the gunshot wound, our baby unharmed and for you… our friends for helping rescue Anna down in Mexico. You are all special and to you, Jamie, I say this… will you be a godmother to Merci?" I then looked at Anna. I hadn't discussed this with her or anyone else, and I swear I saw her eyes fill with what I can only describe as unadulterated pure love… for me.

Jamie started crying but managed to blubber, "Matt, Anna, that's the most beautiful thing ever said to me… I would be honoured and delighted."

It was supposed to be out of earshot, but I heard what Elaine Steele said as she leaned over to Anna to whisper, "Maybe Celia LeFevre's words have struck home? I have never seen Matt look so contented."

She was right. I did, and I am. I also wondered if anything was going to screw up my happiness.

CHAPTER THIRTY-EIGHT

THE LONER

State Trooper Brian Ryder adjusted his smoky-bear as he surveyed the reflection of himself in the full-length hall mirror of the modest two-bedroom bungalow home that until recently he had shared with his now-deceased mother. Glancing down to his highly polished black shoes, he spoke to his reflection. "Only things that fit these days, my shoes and hat." As much as he was sure in the knowledge he was dying from terminal cancer, Ryder averted his gaze from his rheumy eyes set in sunken sockets surrounded by a face showing the tell-tale signs of yellowing skin, the hallmark of serious illness. He was not going to permit any thoughts of self-pity to divert him from his determination to carry out his mission. The trooper made a mental note of how much weight he had lost, all too evident from the loose fit of his Florida Highway Patrol uniform but disregarded that as a minor detail. *Folks will look at the uniform, not the man wearing it*, he thought. *Anyway, I'll only need a few moments to kill the sonofabitch.*

Brian Ryder had always been a loner. A loner through school, in relationships – not that there were any, and right through his service in the Florida Highway Patrol. He had envied the closeness of the two Rs. Arnie Regan and Chuck Roper were closer than Sonny and Cher – before the duo broke up of course. Sometimes he felt like serenading them with a verse from *I Got You, Babe,* but always restrained the thought as it was so out of character for him. Ryder had also admired their strong family backgrounds with supportive wives. He wished he could find someone like that, someone to love and be loved back. Ryder always enjoyed his shifts with either of the two Rs as the relief man when one or the other took leave or was absent through sickness. He knew the feeling wasn't reciprocated as the one 'R' always missed the company of the other 'R,' but it didn't matter to him as he understood, besides, there were still the boys' poker nights when Regan or Roper weren't as close-knit as they were at work. On those nights, Ryder felt part of the team. He knew he owed them as possibly the only man in the whole of the state with nothing to lose. He would be dead soon anyway.

Russo had been separated from his two wise guys once back in Texas. The two henchmen had been taken back to New Jersey on some relatively minor RICO, Racketeer Influenced and Corrupt Organizations Act, charges. The truth was those charges would melt like snow in spring because they had been flipped by the Agent in charge. The promise of witness protection for the two men was the deciding factor seeing they were in a jam. They had no wish to be indicted on felony charges involving Russo's activities, especially those concerning Matt Deal. In the future, they would testify at a Grand Jury hearing to seal their berths in the witness protection programme.

Russo was now in custody in Florida awaiting an arraignment hearing for his part as an accessory in the first-degree murders of the two Florida Highway Patrol troopers Regan and Roper and attempted murders of Matt Deal and Wolfie Jules. Those charges arose in connection to the day his two hitmen Caruso and Messina were killed. The New Jersey *capo* left the Lecanto metropolitan correctional centre escorted by two U.S. Marshals early in the morning. The driver of the centre's prisoner transport van knew he could easily make it to the Northern District of Florida Federal

Courthouse in Tallahassee by 11:30 AM, the appointed time for the arraignment hearing. The driver knew that was particularly so on finding light traffic all the way north up I-75, then even lighter west on I-10 to Tallahassee. He cruised in carefree mode on a bright and warm January day without a cloud in the sky.

Trooper Brian Ryder first checked the online listing for the Federal Courthouse and on seeing the Russo case was listed for eleven-thirty, he checked his Glock service weapon before holstering it. Backing his car out of the garage onto the deserted street, he set off for the courthouse determined to settle matters. On arriving in downtown Tallahassee, Ryder circled the block at the Federal Courthouse location in his nondescript Toyota Prius, noting the ramp which led down to the underground parking lot which the trooper knew was the ramp the correctional centre's van would use. Checking his wristwatch, he saw it was 10:45 AM. Ryder knew it was waiting time, so finding a nearby space, he smoothed the Prius into the kerbside and waited for five minutes.

Ryder hoped his timings were correct and the van would arrive promptly at eleven, allowing thirty minutes for Russo to be searched, booked in, and have a last-minute visit from his lawyer. At precisely 10:56 AM, Ryder got out of his Prius, opened the trunk and removed four Highway Patrol flares usually used to warn traffic at an accident scene. Walking the few yards to the ramp entrance, he set off all four which emitted acrid plumes of reddish-orange smoke. Ryder waited some more with a bullshit cover story in case some innocent bystander should inquire about what was going on. He didn't have to use it. The van drove up and made to turn right into the underground car park when the driver saw State Trooper Ryder in full Highway Patrol uniform. On pulling level with Ryder, the driver powered down his window, but before he could ask, Ryder calmly said, "Nothing to concern yourself. Just a precaution. We have a 10-66 suspicious person sighting down there."

"How long will it take to clear the garage?"

"Ha, how long is a piece of string? Follow me. I'll show you where to park."

Without waiting, Ryder walked off, turned the corner then turned back to make sure the van was following. It was. The trooper gestured to an empty parking space in the road outside the federal building. As the truck parked, Ryder stood on the sidewalk looking up to the top of the imposing stone steps leading to the court entrance. The local TV news crew of one reporter and a cameraman had spotted what was happening and started to make their way down to the sidewalk. Turning his back to the steps, Ryder saw the driver unlock the rear doors of the van allowing the two U.S. Marshals to exit, followed by Russo wearing an orange correctional centre jumpsuit. His arms were handcuffed in front of him with a manacle attached to the handcuff shackles. Using the steps at the back of the van, Russo was too proud to accept a helping hand from the driver as he shuffled to the sidewalk. The Marshal carrying the pump-action twelve-gauge checked around for any suspicious persons. He didn't look at the state trooper.

Ryder unholstered his service Glock with a thirteen-round magazine. He fired thirteen times, twice initially into Russo's head, then the rest into his prone body until Ryder was completely satisfied the *capo* was dead. As the thirteenth round left the chamber, the Marshal's shotgun blew away most of Ryder's face.

As his brain shut down, Ryder experienced an out of body moment. He saw himself speaking his last words on this Earth. "I'm no longer a loner. Every law enforcement officer in the country knows me now." He felt at peace.

"Did you get that?" the local newsman cried out to the cameraman.

"Get what?"

"He said something. Did you record it?"

CHAPTER THIRTY-NINE

THE REUNION

Kappa Alpha fraternity from Georgia Tech held their annual reunion at Myrtle Beach, South Carolina, just as they planned when Conor O'Rourke, their unofficial leader was still alive. Now, there was only Roland Fenney, Brett Angus, Paul Greenslade, and Tim Heath gathered in the three-bedroomed full-service unit of a beach-facing Days Inn. Conor O'Rourke was dead, killed by Matt Deal and Wolfie Jules according to Conor's father, Brendan O'Rourke.

All four were drunk and smoking marijuana, just like in the aftermath of the attack seven years ago. That attack involved the gang rape of Mercy, Deal's daughter. They had agreed with Conor after he told them it was too risky to return to Sandestin, near where they brutally assaulted Mercy at Destin Beach. Not that Conor ever admitted it was a brutal assault.

To him, it was fun and part of growing up. Conor O'Rourke and his group only realised the seriousness of their actions after they learned the girl was in a state of PVS. They had researched the acronym in medical texts, so knew it stood for a persistent vegetative state or post-coma unresponsiveness. They had no clue she had died recently.

Drinking their beers and toking on a joint, it was Tim Heath who drew their attention to the evening news bulletin on the TV. "Shut the fuck up, listen," he yelled. It did the trick as all present watched in silence as the reporter talked into the camera on the steps of Tallahassee Federal Courthouse. The report had made it to the major news channels owing to the identity of the infamous victim.

"Use the TiVo," Fenney said. "Rewind so we can watch from the beginning." Heath used the remote to do it.

"This is Frank Torres of WYBC Tallahassee TV News Station reporting from the federal courthouse in Tallahassee. I have just witnessed the shooting of the New Jersey Mob's capo, Mike Russo, right here outside the courthouse. A man dressed in the Florida Highway Patrol uniform fired a pistol several times at close range, fatally wounding the Mafia boss. That's all we know for now but stay tuned to the channel for

updates. This is Frank Torres of WYBC Tallahassee TV News Station bringing you this breaking news."

"What the fuck!" Greenslade shouted.

"The fuck is… how will this affect us," Heath said.

Fenney was the calm, analytic one out of the bunch. He had dropped out of medical school after realising he needed to qualify as a medical doctor before further study to become a psychiatrist. It was the workings of the human brain that most interested him. He was the odd one out with his passion for climate change and a hippie lifestyle.

"Let's think about this before rushing to judgement. Here's what we know or think we know," Fenney said as the others listened, which they tended to do despite him not chasing wealth like all the others. "Russo is shot, possibly by a cop. We don't know that for sure and even if he is a cop, is he connected to Deal?"

Heath, as impatient as ever snorted. "Mister O'Rourke said Deal murdered Conor. That's good enough for me. Conor's father was tied in with the mob and Russo, we know that much… so it's a good bet Deal is behind Russo's death."

Brett Angus, one of the two lawyers in the frat pack, listened with care before speaking. "You guys forgot something."

"What?" Fenney said.

"Deal and his chick shot dead Russo's hitmen, didn't they?"

"How do you know they were Russo's men," Fenney asked.

"Oh, come on. They were from Jersey… doh," Angus said.

"That's right. I saw that on the news," Greenslade, the other lawyer in their midst, said.

"Right. So, the question is, what do we do about Deal?" Heath asked.

"You mean like a plan?" Fenney asked. "Because if you're planning to snuff him count me out. Besides, tougher people than us have tried and failed. And tell me this… if he wanted to kill us for what happened to his daughter, don't you think he would have done it by now. Maybe he was content after killing Conor, after all, he was the main dude."

Heath said, "Fuck the main dude crap. We were all there and in it together."

"This is getting us nowhere. Don't we have a contact in Destin for some inside info on Deal?" Greenslade said.

"We did, but he's dead too. Wouldn't surprise me if Deal had something to do with that," Brett Angus said.

"Who?" asked Greenslade.

"Captain Stevenson, the cop who lost the DNA," Angus said.

"Wait up, what about the woman cop? The one who took a fancy to you, Roly," Angus said.

"Nah, I don't think she would help," Fenney said.

"Try her, you never know," Greenslade said.

"Okay. I have another idea. I met a guy from Destin on a climate change rally last month. I'll call him too."

SHERIFF

"You know, Matt, I hadn't thought of that. Sandy would be ideal," Anna said.

"It would be a reward for her getting her business masters. Goodness knows, she's studied part-time a long time for it. And it will help take her mind off all that's happened, especially Bobby," I said.

"Jamie can run the gym side of things, and Sandy can use the office upstairs as general manager, don't you think? One thing, though."

"What's that?"

"We need to move my server out and back to the bunker."

I knew she was right. The server Anna mentioned was the one she had built when I was in England. She did that to help me with my predicament there, after I was charged with the murder of Tommy Etchwell, building her server to camouflage her identity and location. Owing to her encryption skills learnt at NASA before I met her, there wasn't a digital file or footprint that was safe from Anna's probing. She was a denizen of the darknet if those skills were called for.

I thought about what she was suggesting before I replied, "Couldn't have put it better myself. The new arrangement will also give you some rest. You need it after the ordeals in Texas and Mexico. I can move the server before Sandy takes the position as I guess it makes sense for her to move into our apartment. I will also move the bag. The one we brought back from Mexico."

"Well, I thought Jamie and Pat could move into the top floor apartment. Sandy can either use the other bedroom or carry on living with her folks," Anna said.

"No problem with that as long as it means you get plenty of rest," I said.

"Talking about rest, what about you? How's the thumb and finger now, not to mention a cracked rib and broken tooth?"

"Tough as old boots. I'm fine. Heard from Ellie?"

"Yes, she's taking some leave in El Paso before she starts officially there in the Bureau," Anna said.

"I bet a certain Mexican colonel is also in El Paso." I smiled.

"That's no bet. It's a fact. She told me," Anna said.

"Do you think …?"

"I do, and I also hope so. They are meant for each other, "Anna said. "By the way, guess what Ellie said about you at the dinner the other night."

"I hope it was clean."

"It was, you dirty-minded scoundrel. She said you have never looked as contented."

"No surprise there, I am contented. I have you, and we are going to have a beautiful baby daughter." I paused before asking, "You want to hear my news?"

"Of course."

"The Walton County Chamber of Commerce has asked me to consider running for Sheriff," I said.

"That's great, and will you?"

"Probably. I think what persuaded me was what they had to say about corruption in the police department. Mary Smyth was the one who called me. She's a big chief on the chamber of commerce and local politics. Anyway, she said it was a problem going back to the Captain Stevenson days and before that. Well, that did ring my bell," I said.

"I'm sure it did," Anna said.

"And then when I got her reaction to my way of doing things, it confirmed I wanted to do it."

"Your way?" Anna asked.

"Yeah, an active sheriff. One who doesn't sit behind a desk eating doughnuts and getting fatter by the day. I'll be out there in the front line leading by example." I could feel an inner glow as I spoke.

"That forest green uniform will look sexy with your red hair." Anna laughed.

"You have a thing about me in uniform. Let me tell you that sometimes I will be in mufti doing my detective bit," I said.

"Of course, Detective Matt Deal, just as long as you wear that uniform to bed sometimes to please your wife to be."

CHAPTER FORTY-ONE

SITTING TARGET

The Kappa Alpha frat pals had decided to get their fill of more beers at the Lucky Clover, a Myrtle Beach Irish Bar known for the most extended happy hour in town. Luckily for Roland Fenney but not so lucky for the bar owner, the new bartender fell for the oldest trick in the book when Fenney asked him to use the phone at the far side of the bar to make a local call. Instead, and out of earshot of the new guy, he called long distance to Destin. "Mervyn, it's me, Roly, you know, from the rally."

"Hey man, how you doing?"

"Good, yeah good. Listen, can you do me a favour?"

"What is it?"

"Your mom knows all that's going on in your part of the world, I remember you telling me about her."

"Yeah, she's the Pres of the local chamber of commerce. What do you wanna know?"

"A guy called Matt Deal. He has a gym in Destin. Just wanna know if she's heard anything about him," Roly said.

"You a mind reader or something?"

"No, why?" Roly said.

"She mentioned him only yesterday. Said she was thinking of asking him to run for Sheriff here in Walton County. Why? What is he to you?"

The line went dead.

Roly Fenney summoned his pals over to an empty table at the end of the large bar. Once he told them of the new development, it was Heath who spoke first. "That's it then."

"What's it?" Fenney said.

"I think he means he's a sitting target," Greenslade said.

"Count me out, if you are saying what I think you're saying," Fenney said.

"Hey! Fuck you, if you want to take a chance that Deal is going to let us be, then let me tell you I don't buy it," Heath said.

"I'm with you," Greenslade said. "We vote on it. Majority vote means as always, we all agree. Those were Conor's rules, and if we don't want to end up like him, we do it his way. The Kappa Alpha way," he added.

The four young men stared into their beers, paused for a few moments before three of them said, "Aye."

Roland Fenney left the table, leaving his frat friends Brett Angus, Paul Greenslade, and Tim Heath to wonder about how best to protect their future interests.

Fenney wrestled with his conscience as the weeks went by. He had always felt wrong about what he and his so-called friends had inflicted upon the pretty young blonde on that Destin beach all those years ago. But he knew he'd feel a lot worse locked up for years if there was ever a conviction for rape and sexual assault. Worse still if Deal ever got to kill him. Then he laughed at the idiocy of that thought, but he decided to call the friendly cop in Florida.

"Hey! How are you these days?" Fenney said.

"Who is this?"

"Roly. Roland Fenney."

"You're kidding me, right?"

"No, it's me. Remember me?"

"I do. You and the other frat kids. You know you should all be still serving jail time for what you did to that kid. What was her name?" *As if I had forgotten,* she thought.

"Mercy."

"That's it. How could I forget? So, what do you want?"

"I heard her father is going to be the new sheriff, is that right?"

"Yeah, I heard that too, but the election isn't for another four months yet. So, who knows?" Deputy Sheriff Christine Solley said.

"Okay, thanks and by the way, thanks for the friendly face when I was in your jail."

"Just doing my job. We are human, you know. Hey, before you go, I never did find out why you guys beat that rap," Solley lied.

"The DNA got lost. The DA dropped all charges," Fenney said.

I know that, you dumb asshole, it was me who made it disappear from the property cage, Solley thought as she finished the call.

Deputy Sheriff Christine Solley had served ten years with Walton County. She had been hired by Captain Stevenson, the former chief of detectives responsible for investigating the assault on Mercy Deal. He had been a district patrol lieutenant at that time. Solley was a thick-set, heavy-boned woman who had been a track and field scholar in her younger days. She was plain but not ugly and was single through choice, not through being unattractive. She did have one asset that Stevenson took a fancy to, and that was her big boobs.

Solley didn't know it, but Stevenson was often making the old, tired joke in male company when asked why certain females were selected above others for appointment to Deputy Sheriff. He never ceased to guffaw at his line of, "The one with the biggest tits," as if he had invented the sexist joke. It was common knowledge Stevenson had a drinking problem after the death of his wife. It was in Solley's arms and ample bosom he sought solace, and she didn't mind. She liked his southern charm and gentlemanly ways and didn't give a fig he was quite a bit older than her. She started to fall for him, so much so they started dating… and making plans for both on his retirement. Those plans were daydreams. Talk of a new life together in Ecuador – a new country and a fresh start.

Daydreams until Stevenson investigated the Mercy Deal case and until he was bribed to lose the evidence in the case by Brendan O'Rourke, the father of one of the suspects. Initially, Solley was reluctant to help him lose the DNA evidence but blinded by love, she eventually agreed when she was next on the property cage roster. Stevenson soon fixed that. The DNA went missing, and not even Stevenson knew where it had gone. But Solley did. She kept it as a kind of insurance policy in the garage refrigerator of her modest home, ironically close to Destin Beach, the scene of the brutal assault on Mercy. Now, Fenney had called. What to do, if anything?

Let sleeping dogs lie or… if Deal gets elected Sheriff, will he start sniffing around? Should I blackmail the suspects? Their folks are all rich, and it'll make up for that life in Ecuador I never had with Stevenson. Anyways, Bahamas sounds better, or maybe Panama City?

Solley made a call the next day before she reported for duty.

DEPUTY SHERIFF SOLLEY

The reception phone rang in Matt Deal's Big Deal Gym. Sandy took the call and placed it straight through to Matt in the upstairs office. She waited for Matt to pick up before she replaced her phone on the cradle. These were the last few weeks of her reception duties after Matt and Anna informed her of the new management structure. Sandy was delighted to hear the news.

"Yes, Matt Deal here," I said. "Who is this?"

"Christine Solley. Deputy Sheriff Solley of Walton County P.D."

"What can I do for you?" I asked.

"I hear on the grapevine you are going to run for Sheriff."

"And... if that is true..." I didn't get to finish.

"I'm the union rep, so I know what's what when it comes to Walton P.D. It might be worth your while meeting up. That's if the rumours are true about you running," she said.

"That sounds persuasive, Deputy," I said.

"Christine, please call me Christine, at least until you get elected," she said.

"Okay, Christine. What do you have in mind?"

"You like fishing?"

"Sometimes."

"Deep-sea kind, I mean. My father has a forty-foot boat all rigged out. You ever catch swordfish?" she asked.

"Matter of fact, I have. That's one hell of a fish to catch."

"You bet. Just say when and I'll arrange it."

"Okay. I will. Give me your cell number," I said.

She did, and I wrote it down on the desk pad in front of me.

"Okay. Got it. I have a few things to attend to at my gym, so I'll call you in a few days to arrange things. Is that okay?"

Anna and Jamie were in the office, with Anna taking Jamie through all the admin stuff Jamie needed to know in her new role as chief instructor in the gym business. Anna broke off to speak. "What was that all about?"

I told her what had been discussed and that was when Jamie got all excited. "Deep-sea fishing. Wow! I love it."

"You been before?" I asked.

"Yeah, three or four times when I worked in Corpus Christi."

"Matt, take Jamie with you," Anna said.

"What about you?" I asked.

"I have enough morning sickness now without seasickness on top of that." She smiled.

"Wise choice, I guess," I said. "Okay, Jamie, it looks like you and me, but what about Pat?"

"Depends if he's back from New Orleans."

"Is he still searching for the right tractor unit?" Anna asked.

"You know Pat, it has to be the exact fit for his shopping list," Jamie said.

"I thought a big truck was a big truck. Won't wheels, tyres, an engine and cab do?" I quipped.

"Matt, don't show your ignorance. There are trucks on the one hand and on the other, there are the right trucks," Anna said.

About two weeks or so later I still hadn't heard from Solley, so I called her because I was starting to look forward to a great day's fishing out in the Gulf of Mexico and Jamie was forever asking me when. She was settling into the routine of her new position at the gym business and liking the new accommodation arrangements now she had moved into our old apartment on the top floor of the gym building. Sandy was also happy in her new role as general manager, utilising all her newly learnt business administration knowledge. She had decided to carry on living with her family, just the other side of Destin.

I was also curious about what Solley was going to say about me and the election, especially seeing she had some insights into that P.D. as a union rep. There was also another reason I called her. Mary Smyth was starting to apply pressure on me to decide whether I was going to run for Sheriff in the election as the nomination deadline was looming, yet the election itself was still a few months away. I felt the wheels were grinding, so I made the call.

"Hey, Christine, it's me, Matt Deal. Are we still on for this fishing trip?"

"That's weird. I'd just written a note to remind me to call you. Yeah, I have my roster details now so what about one week today? I have a day off on that day, so that suits me fine."

"Sounds good to me. Do I need to bring anything?"

"Not much. The boat's rigged out with reels, tackle, and bait will be on board too. You will need sunblock, shades, a cooler sixpack and some food. Other than that, just you."

"I'm bringing a friend. Is that okay with you?" I sensed a moment's hesitation which really ought to have set off an alarm bell but it didn't, so I added, "One of my gym instructors. She just loves deep-sea fishing, so I found it hard to say no once she asked me."

"It's fine," Solley said in a flat monotone.

"Time and place, then?"

"Huh?" Solley seemed distracted.

"Meeting place," I said to give her a clue.

"Sorry, I'm not with it today. Destin Harbor. Make your way to the marina and ask anybody where the *Aurora* is docked. Five o'clock sharp."

"It won't be daylight until about seven."

"I know, but you guys can help me, so we are ready to sail just before dawn breaks, and you get oriented with the boat before we sail."

"Makes sense. May I ask if you have a skipper's ticket."

"Of course, I've had one for five years now. See you next week, right?"

"You got it. I'm looking forward to it too. Before you go, can you give me a heads up as to what you want to talk about?"

"Sure. I can help you win the election."

"How so?"

"That's why we need to talk in person. Let me just say you won't be disappointed."

"Sounds okay to me. See you next week. Bye, Christine."

CHAPTER FORTY-THREE

VIABLE PLAN

Christine Solley had not yet decided about her exact plans when Matt Deal and his friend sailed on the *Aurora* next week. She wasn't sure she could carry out a serious crime, a notion the deputy laughed at when she thought about the obstruction of justice in losing the DNA evidence in the Mercy Deal case. She corrected herself. Can I kill two people, Deal and his friend? And then got to wondering – who is she? This is a complication.

The call from Deal had interrupted what she was in the middle of – preparing a blackmail demand to lose that DNA forever. She'd mulled this over many times since the Fenney phone call and decided it was a viable plan. Viable because the statute of time limitations never expired in Florida when the victim was a minor, which Mercy Deal was at the tender age of fifteen when she was assaulted. The rapists' families would pay dearly to bury this secret once and for all. Wouldn't they?

Who to send it to? That was the only question left hanging. No point in sending the same demand note to all of them; that only increased the chance of detection. Deputy Sheriff Solley worked swiftly with her latex-gloved hands, sitting at the kitchen table in her Destin home. Cutting from old newspaper headlines then using glue to paste them onto the page ripped out from a dollar store notepad, she conjured up a six by nine inches chilling message:

I HAVE DNA U THINK WAS LOST

PAY ME IN USED BILLS NO HIGHER THAN 50

DO NOT CALL POLICE

I AM SERIOUS

DO NOTHING I WILL CONTACT YOU

HAVE MONEY REDY IN XCAHNGE FOR RETURN OF DNA

She stood back from her handiwork and spotted the spelling mistakes but decided to leave it be as she thought it looked more genuine. For the next hour she interrogated the Internet until she found the answer to the 'who.'

Tasks complete, her thoughts wandered to Deal and the fishing trip one week away. She didn't tell him she had three days off because that was none of his business. It was also none of his business what she planned to do on the days before she met Deal and his lady friend at Destin Harbor. None of his business because whatever those frat kids did and what she was planning wouldn't bring the poor girl back from the dead. Life's a bitch, and some.

"You sure about running for sheriff?" Anna said after we had finished our delicious sushi meal I had bought on the way home.

"Yes, why?" I said.

"Just in case you don't know already, or Mary Smyth hasn't clued you in, it's not like a sheriff out in the backwoods. You know, like one of those Reacher novels you keep reading. They are loners roaming around their one-eyed town with one or two deputies and maybe get to investigate two or three crimes every year. Walton County has a multi-million-dollar budget. As Sheriff, you are more like a Fortune 500 CEO."

"Oh, knock it off, Anna. No need to exaggerate."

"Okay, I am overstating things, but you will be a figurehead with all kinds of people reporting to you."

"Such as?"

Anna brought up the Walton County website on her laptop and started to read aloud, "The Walton County Sheriff's Office is a full-service, state-accredited public safety agency that serves the entirety of Walton County, Florida. WCSO employs approximately three-hundred and seventy law enforcement employees, including roughly two-hundred and fifty certified deputy sheriffs and one-hundred and twenty administrative employees. The Walton County Sheriff's Office provides full-time law enforcement services in the four main districts of Walton County. Also, the Walton County Sheriff's Office protects the Walton County Courthouse, the Walton County Courthouse Annex and Walton County Schools …"

"Right, I get the picture," I interrupted.

"There's more," Anna said seeming like she wanted to get it all off her chest.

"So, you're saying you either don't want me to run, or I'm not capable. Which is it?"

"Neither, Matt Deal. I simply want you to be happy, and I'm not convinced this position is best for you and your capabilities. Don't forget. I *know* you." Anna continued to stare at the screen in front of her. I saw her click the mouse a few times and then she spoke again. "The Sheriff isn't merely running the law enforcement in the county, he's at the top of a chain of command. Listen to me." Anna sensed I was in a huff. It must have been the look of exasperation on my face. "Look at this chart."

She showed me an organisational chart, and I saw where she was coming from. There was a Public Affairs Coordinator, the Chief Deputy, a Director of Emergency Services, the IT chief, and the heads of Crime Prevention, Criminal Intel, Communications, Fire Rescue, Animal Services, and the Director of Jail Operations all reporting to the WCSO Sheriff. And that was before my eyes moved down to law enforcement *per se* with a Director of Law Enforcement overseeing the Criminal Investigations Bureau, among all the other parts that go to comprise a modern police department.

Almost like Anna could read my mind, she pointed to the next organisational chart below the one I was staring at. Her finger hovered over the title of Criminal Investigations Bureau Chief reporting only to the Sheriff. Not only that, the post was by appointment by the Sheriff. There was no bloody election. I knew she was right. That was the job that suited me, but I had already told Mary Smyth I would run for election.

"Anna, I think you could be right, but and there are two things. First, I have told Mary Smyth I will run, and the necessary paperwork has been filed. Two, what she said to me about cleaning up the corruption is the only reason I ever agreed to do it. Make that three, there's a good chance I can find out what happened to the missing DNA if I start rooting out the bad cops."

"Matt, I get it. I really do. As I said, I just want you to be happy."

"I know, and I thank you for it. I tell you what, let me think about it. The candidates aren't announced for another few weeks. If I change my mind, I'll withdraw before it's official. The fishing trip gives me the ideal thinking time. That clean ocean air will relax me and clear my head."

"Matt, I love you and never forget, whatever you decide, I'm there right with you. By the way, put the next scan in your diary," Anna said as she took my hand and placed it on her expanding belly.

CHAPTER FORTY-FOUR

BEL AIR

"Hey Lana, it's me, Chrissie," Deputy Sheriff Christine Solley said down the phone.

"Great to hear from you. What on earth are you up to these days? Not heard a peep from you in aeons," Lana Anderson said.

"Same. Still a cop in Destin."

"Man trouble?" Lana asked.

"No, nothing like that. I'm coming up to Atlanta in a few days on police business, so I thought it would be great to meet up again."

"That is so cool. Look, Marty won't be here in all probability as he's on-site in Wisconsin and I have no reliable sitter, so why don't I cook something up? We can drink some wine and catch up."

"That's great. You still live in Bel Air?"

"Yes. When do you plan to come?" Lana asked.

"I'll call you the day before and then again when I'm close by," Solley said.

Chrissie Solley had no police business to attend to in Atlanta, nor any other legitimate reason to go there. Deputy Sheriff Solley, just Chrissie to her friend Lana, set off for Atlanta anticipating it would take a little over five hours' driving. She knew precisely where the Greenslade's lived. Paul Greenslade was still single and living with his parents in their five-bedroomed home on a gated community just outside of Atlanta, Bel Air it was called. She felt it was a good omen that her best friend from high school also lived in the same community, making it easier for her to approach the Greenslade home. Halfway there, she stopped at a gas station to fill up her Honda Accord and grab a coffee while inside paying for the gas. She made one more stop to check the package alongside her before driving on to her friend's home. Satisfied the demand note was securely wrapped in the plain brown paper weighted down with a piece of scrap lead she had found near to Destin Marina, she called Lana. "Traffic's light. I might be there in about forty minutes."

Precisely forty-five minutes later, Solley drove into the expansive Anderson's front yard, expensively landscaped with shrubs, trees, and rocky area resembling an alpine garden. The drive was asphalt, not cheap cement, with expensive-looking red pavers leading from the two-car garage to the white front door of the two-storey house. Solley had noticed all the homes in this community were similarly bedecked with mature yards with plenty of shrubberies.

Parking the white Accord and before she shoved the automatic shift to P, Solley collected the brown parcel measuring six by nine and placed it into her overnight bag. That was when she heard kids' voices. "Aunty Chrissie, Aunty Chrissie," Lana's children cried.

"Karen, take the bag. Carol, let Aunty Chrissie get through the front door. She doesn't want to trample you," Lana said, laying down the law.

"Oh my! They are so big. I hope the tees I bought fit."

"Don't worry about that. The girls are pleased to see you as if you didn't know already. Me too, give me a big hug, Chrissie."

Hugs over, Lana took Chrissie through to the expansive kitchen where the smell of good cooking pervaded the air.

"That smells delicious," Chrissie said.

"Spag bol, my speciality," Lana smiled, "with a special secret Italian ingredient."

"Give."

"Well, actually it's a special selection of herbs I found in a local Italian deli. That and two bottles of Italian merlot. I hope you are hungry."

"Matter of fact, I am."

"Look, let's eat after we catch up a bit but first let me show you your room. I'll take that," Lana said as she reached for Chrissie's overnight bag.

"That's okay. It's not heavy," Chrissie said, tightening her grip on the bag.

"You have the English Crown Jewels in there?" Lana laughed.

"Just the tees for the girls, my overnight and my running stuff."

"You still run?" Lana asked. "I thought you'd left all that behind."

"Just to keep in shape. I see so many cops gone to seed because they stop exercising. Not, me, girl."

"You plan to take a run here then?"

"Later, before I go to sleep. It will be cooler then too."

"Count me out. Remind me to give you the alarm code so you can let yourself out and get back in again without rousing the neighbourhood."

"Thanks. You know what they say about the best-laid plans?"

"Yeah, so after food and wine you might change your mind?"

"Who knows? I do like my daily run, so I'll probably make an effort."

"Come on, I'll show you the room. There's an *en suite* if you want to shower before dinner."

"Wait up, let me dig out the tees for the girls," Chrissie said as she pulled out two tee shirts with 'Reel Destin' and a shark emblazoned on the front.

"Cute. I'm sure the girls will love them."

"Where are they, by the way?"

"Through there, glued to the TV." Lana nodded towards an open door off the hall. It was another large room filled with green sofas, matching comfortable chairs, and a huge flat-screen TV mounted on the wall. "You can give them the tees later."

Lana took Chrissie to her comfortable guest bedroom complete with walk-in shower and left her be so she could freshen up before dinner was served.

Lana decided to let the girls eat earlier so she could have a grown-up's chat with her old friend over several glasses of red wine. Once the girls had finished, Lana cajoled them into their pre-bedtime routine of brushing teeth and hair before reading them a story. Still, on the occasion of the visit of Aunty Chrissie, the girls unanimously clamoured for a different voice to read to them. The pleading worked so Chrissie sat at the foot of Carol's bed, she being the younger of the two, while Karen propped herself up on a pillow in her bed, listening intently to Chrissie reciting from their favourite book, *The Lion, the Witch and the Wardrobe*. Three chapters in Chrissie saw the girls were falling to sleep, so kissing them both goodnight, she closed the book, turned off the light set on a low table between the girls' beds and turned to leave the bedroom where she saw Lana beckoning her over. "You look like you have been doing that forever," she said.

"No. I enjoy it because it reminds me of when I was their age when life was easy, and I had no clue as to the meaning of the word 'complications.'"

"I'll drink to that. Come, let's eat," Lana said.

Chrissie enjoyed the meal but limited herself to only two glasses of the fruity Italian merlot, reminding herself about the real reason for her visit.

After much chit chat in the form of both catching up and reminiscences, Lana excused herself. "Chrissie, I'm sorry, but I need to go to bed. I drank way too much. Can you remember how to operate the alarm?"

"Yes, no problem. Get yourself off to sleep. Tomorrow's another day," Chrissie said.

CHAPTER FORTY-FIVE

RUNNING

Christine Solley waited two hours, watching some mindless TV show in the living room, before she decided to venture up to her bedroom where she changed into her running outfit, a black sports bra, black running pants, and donned her Nike shoes. Reaching into her bag, she pulled out a black beanie and placed it on her head, first making sure she had tucked in any loose strands of hair under the hat. After that, Solley put on her black running gloves. Last of all, she picked up the package wrapped in brown paper that she needed to deliver to the Greenslade residence. In complete silence, the guest made her way to the front door, keyed in the code on the alarm box, slipped the spare key Lana had entrusted to her inside her left glove while carrying the package in her gloved right hand.

She started running the second she got out of the front door, confident the mental map she had inside her head would guide her to her destination. It did. The Greenslade home was on the street running parallel to her friend's road. She made a left after two-hundred yards, followed by a right after a thousand yards, then Deputy Sheriff Christine Solley confirmed her destination when she saw the prominent house number on the mailbox – 3914.

Pausing to catch her breath, she first looked up and down the street. Nothing. Looking at the two-storey house, she saw no lights. It was two in the morning, so that didn't surprise her. Sneaking up the driveway, she concluded the large downstairs front bay window was the target. Solley cautiously moved across the manicured lawn until she felt close enough to the target. With muscle memory kicking in from her pentathlon days, she held the package in the shot put fashion then powered it through the air at the glass window.

Not waiting, she turned and started running… hard and fast. She heard the glass shatter and ran even faster at the sound of the house alarm system. After five-hundred yards back in the reverse direction, she stopped to duck behind some shrubs at the front of a house. She listened and waited. After three minutes or so, the alarm stopped. She crouched there for another thirty minutes, and no one arrived at the Greenslade house. Solley, with all her cop training and experience, knew that was good. The Greenslade family must have read the note and decided to do nothing in terms of calling the police. She was confident they would take the necessary steps to protect their son. Thinking time over, she stood up and ran back to her friend's home before climbing into bed and sleeping for six hours before she set off back to Destin and a fishing trip appointment with Deal the next day.

The sound of breaking glass followed by the home alarm woke Paul Greenslade and his parents, Aaron and Camelia. All three huddled in the kitchen, taking turns in reading the note. Camelia was first to speak. "We need to call the police."

Aaron sharply said, "We do no such thing."

"Paul added, "I agree. The cops may find stuff we don't want them to find. Another thing, and I've not told you about this. We had a meeting recently, and we are all convinced it's Matt Deal who's after us all."

"What do you mean, son?" Aaron said.

"He killed Conor. Well, that's according to Conor's father."

"We can't ask his father now, though. I read his obituary. Got himself killed down in Mexico. Some suggest it was connected to drug trafficking."

"Don't you see, Pop? That all makes sense," Paul said, adding, "Jack Russo got killed too after he was arrested in Mexico."

"The Jack Russo?" his father said. Aaron Greenslade was a hotshot lawyer in Atlanta and knew full well who Jack Russo was. Paul was now a junior partner in the law firm.

Greenslade Senior turned to his wife. "Camelia, go back to sleep, please. These are things you don't need to hear about."

Sighing she agreed, but only because she knew the veil of secrecy was about to be drawn across certain dealings of her husband like many previous occasions. She was resigned to that situation, knowing it helped their lifestyle.

Watching his wife retire to bed, Aaron Greenslade said, "Makes a lot of sense, I agree. Deal is the connection. His daughter is assaulted. It appears he killed Conor then he kills two of Russo's hitmen before he gets involved with Russo and Brendan down in Mexico. I'm only guessing about Mexico, but I bet I'm right. I can feel it."

"Did you know Russo was extradited to Florida?"

"No."

"He was, and then he got shot dead on the steps of the federal courthouse in Tallahassee. Some state trooper shot him."

"That's where his daughter is in hospital and where he killed Russo's hitmen, right?"

"Damn right, and that's why the guys and I think Deal is coming for all of us."

"Maybe, but why this blackmail note if it's him? I don't get it."

"Blood money before he kills us all. Roland Fenney is asking around down in Destin."

"Roly? What's he found out if anything?"

"There's a rumour Deal's going to run for Sheriff."

"That could be the way out."

"What do you mean, Pop?" Paul said.

"Let me think on it. I know someone who I think can help. Now, forget this happened and don't say a word to the others. Get some sleep, and we'll talk tomorrow at the office, or I should say, later today."

CHAPTER FORTY-SIX

HOLD ALL CALLS

About the same time Deputy Sheriff Solley parked her white Accord outside her modest bungalow home in Destin, Aaron Greenslade had attended to the important business in his calendar. He used the phone on his desk to inform his PA to hold all calls until further notice. Greenslade's law practice encompassed both civil and criminal cases, mostly humdrum but with the odd high-profile case. One of his more high-profile civil cases was acting for Benjamin Turner, a self-styled pastor with no divinity training whatsoever who led a 'church' of blind followers who believed in all he preached.

Most of those followers were Neo-Nazis, and most of them were bikers. They revelled in the pastor's anti-federal missives together with his proclamation that Adolf Hitler was the most recent manifestation of the Messiah. The city of Atlanta had tried to close his 'church' only for Greenslade to successfully argue that to do so would be a breach of his fundamental constitutional rights. Greenslade knew Turner's flock had dwindled to about forty hard-core bikers. He believed, from all he knew, that this was the man who, combined with his outlaw bikers, could eliminate the threat from Deal once and for all.

Greenslade called his chief investigator using a burner cell phone as he didn't want any records of what he was about to set in motion. The tall, lean investigator, Chuck Murphy, ambled into his boss's office after knocking on the door and hearing, "Come."

Handing Murphy a file containing names, locations and photographs, Greenslade said, "Go talk to Benjamin Turner. The man with the red hair must disappear for good. Got it?"

Murphy looked inside the file briefly before holding up the photo of Matt Deal. "Him?"

"Yes, and don't let Turner know this is from me. That's a must. Tell him any old BS. And tell him thirty-thousand will be transferred to his account once I know he's got rid of that guy."

"You got it," Murphy said.

"Chuck, this conversation never happened. You can go now."

Once Murphy had left the office, Aaron Greenslade buzzed through to his PA. "Send Paul up here," he said.

His son entered a few minutes later and was instructed to say nothing to anyone about the blackmail note, Deal or any related matter.

Before Paul left, his father said, "Did your mother arrange for the window to be fixed?"

"Yes, she did. I called her earlier."

"Okay, that's all, Paul."

"Yes, sir," Paul said with sincere deference to his father and employer.

CHAPTER FORTY-SEVEN

CLEAR BLUE WATERS

Dawn was breaking as the *Aurora* sailed out of Destin Harbor with its crew of Deputy Sheriff Christine Solley, Sheriff-elect Matt Deal and Jamie. They had all been on board the boat for the past two hours, and under Solley's supervision they had checked all the equipment for a day's fishing and undergone safety drills. Solley had then given her guests a quick tour of the forty-footer so, as she joked, "Now you know the front from the back." It was more of a reassurance to them that her father's boat was fully equipped with ship-to-shore radio, radar, GPS, depth finder, one inflatable life raft, several rescue flares and life jackets, a gas stove and a refrigerator. The aim was to try to find and catch a swordfish and to do that, Solley knew they would have to venture at least thirty miles offshore out into the clear blue waters of the Gulf of Mexico to be in with a realistic chance. Even at this early hour, the sun was beginning to warm all it touched under a clear, bright blue sky.

It was a great feeling getting out of the harbour. I could feel the warmth of the sun's rays already, so I was glad I brought the sunblock as I'd need it later. There was a gentle swell which I found relaxing, and the smell of the ozone on the ocean breeze was better than any tonic known to man. The deputy seems to know what she's doing. This will be some trip. I hope we catch a swordfish for Jamie's sake. I know what the hell of a catch it is, but she has got to experience that. Fingers crossed.

My mind went back to old times in England, and I recalled how much I missed the sun on my back and the smell of the ocean when I was an NCA detective. I thought about Mickey Fretwell too. He replaced Elaine Steele as my partner on the NCA. Poor bugger took a bullet for me. Last I heard he was now out of a wheelchair and on the road to a full recovery. Isn't life right, I thought as I turned about to watch the fast-disappearing shoreline. I was mesmerised by the foamy wake of the boat with its big V-8 twin-engine churning up the water. I was lost in a world that was now complete with Anna and a baby girl on the way. I felt myself smiling even when I recalled the memory of Mercy. It was all the good bits I remembered and not my sweet daughter in the hospital or later when machines were keeping her breathing.

I was still a lucky man, I told myself. Then I realised all bitterness towards those kids who had so grossly violated Mercy's body was dissipating. Maybe Celia Le Fevre and Elaine Steele had cast a spell on me? I laughed at the thought and made a firm decision. I would run for sheriff. I wondered when Christine would talk to me about that.

"Matt." I heard Jamie's voice. Turning back towards the bow and the wheelhouse, I saw Jamie with sunblock in her hand. "Do you mind?" she said. "I can't reach all of my back."

"Sure," I said. "Give it to me." She was right. It was now about ten in the morning, and the sun was climbing higher. Jamie was wearing shorts and a halter top. She gave me the sunblock and turned her back to me then untied the top, freeing the loose knot at the nape of her neck. Jamie was standing on deck naked from the waist up, as I massaged the lotion into her back and shoulders. I could not avoid thinking this was something I would have run a mile away from only a short time ago. I confess I admired her. Jamie had beautiful clear brown skin, and as my hands worked down her back to her waist and hips, I realised what a sexy body she had. I did feel a twinge but dismissed it, thinking, *I can now understand Pat, but I'll stick with my beautiful Anna, thank you.*

Jamie turned to face me. I caught a quick glimpse of her small boobs. Yes, small but perfectly formed. She smiled on seeing my expression as if she knew what I was thinking. I was pleased, and the real reason I felt glad was that I had finally come to recognise Jamie truly did feel like a woman and took a natural pleasure in a man admiring her body. Nothing wrong with that. I was happy for her and Pat.

Jamie reached the nape of her slender neck to tie up her halter top. As she did so, she said, "Your turn."

I was dressed in only shorts, having already removed my tee shirt. Shorts meant I had given my Glock to Jamie on boarding the *Aurora* for safekeeping in her bag. She also kept my windbreaker jacket in her purse. I handed Jamie the sunblock and turned my back to her. She smothered my back and shoulders with lotion, lingering on knots in my muscles while she rhythmically massaged my back with her long fingers. "You need Thai massage," she said. I did not answer at first.

Then I had a thought. "Jamie. That's a great idea. Why don't you start up Thai massage at the gym?"

"I will, but do I need to ask Sandy?"

"As a courtesy, yes, but Anna and I will have a word with her so by the time you mention it, she will no doubt agree."

Jamie turned me around having finished massaging my back and kissed me flush on the cheek. "Thank you, Matt."

I knew I had a real good friend in Jamie… "Matt!" I heard Jamie scream.

I turned to see what the scream was about, and saw Solley holding her service pistol. "Whatever this is about, I don't think you should do this," I said, and the calm in my voice surprised me.

"Kill you, you mean?"

"That's what I surmise from you holding a gun in your hand. By the way who's driving the boat?"

"Steering, not driving. No one. It's on autopilot."

To the side of Solley's considerable bulk – in comparison to the slender Jamie – I saw Jamie hop into the wheelhouse then again into a storage area in the bow. I saw her bend over but couldn't make out what she was reaching for, so I carried on talking. "Why kill me?"

"I can't take any chances."

"About what? You're not making any sense."

"You as sheriff."

"I'm not elected yet."

"You will be. I know it… unless…"

Stupid question but I needed to engage her because I could see what Jamie had planned and thought it would work. "Unless what?"

"You're dead."

"Look, let's start from the beginning here because I have no idea why you want me out of the way. If you're going to shoot me with that thing, then at least give me the satisfaction of knowing why."

"It was me who made the DNA disappear in your daughter's case. They got off because of me. If you are elected, I know damn well you will never stop investigating both the case and the disappearance of the DNA evidence."

"It was Captain Stevenson who made the evidence disappear after he was bribed by Brendan O'Rourke, with some help from Jack Hughes along the way."

"You think?"

"I know."

"Ha! You know squat. Did you know Stevenson and I were lovers?"

"No," I said, mentally urging Jamie to act soon. I thought she was nearly ready.

"Well, Deal, we were, and what's more…"

Solley stopped talking. She was still forming words when she fell forward onto the deck in front of me, clutching her gun. A spear was sticking out of her back. I had watched as Jamie fired a band-type speargun she must have found at the boat's bow.

Jamie came running through the wheelhouse onto the deck. "Is she dead?" she said without a trace of emotion.

Before I turned her over, I released the pistol from Solley's grasp. She had that mask of death on her face. Her mouth was open as if she wanted to finish what she wanted to say to me. Instead of words, she bubbled up a red froth accompanied by a shallow rasping. She was dead or as good as. I knew that when I saw the barbed tip of the speargun sticking out of her chest.

Jamie and I stood there for what seemed like a long time. I'm sure it was only seconds. I said, "Thanks." It sounded stupid, so I hugged her instead, adding, "How can I ever repay you?"

"Get us back to shore, for one," she said, smiling.

"I will. We will have to report this, of course."

"Of course."

CHAPTER FORTY-EIGHT

DESTIN MARINE UNIT

I managed to set the *Aurora* in the right direction, knowing which point of the compass we needed to aim for, but I was no expert at navigating a boat like this through the ocean. The twin V-8 engine did its part, and as I held the wheel, I asked Jamie to see if she could raise anyone on the ship to shore radio, preferably the Coastguard or the Destin Harbor Master. After about an hour's sailing, Jamie made contact. It was the Coastguard shore station. They had a cutter in the area and told us they would radio it and get the skipper to instigate a search pattern.

It took another two hours before the cutter found us. The captain launched an inflatable for two of his crew to board us. On climbing aboard the *Aurora* from the small inflatable, I was disconcerted to see both ratings had pistols drawn. One covered

Jamie and me, while the other secured the inflatable to the *Aurora's* stern. Once the second rating joined us at the wheelhouse, the first carried out a swift examination of Solley's lifeless body. He radioed the captain, and we heard the cutter's captain say, "Arrest both. Handcuff them and take them to Destin."

The older of the two U.S. Coastguard ratings said, "You heard him. Show me your hands then place them together like this," as he made a front handcuff position gesture.

"Is no one going to ask me what happened?" I said.

"Yes, not us, though. We will hand you over to the Destin Marine Unit."

"That's the police, right?"

"Correct. That's usually the case if someone gets killed."

The man had no humour. After handcuffing Jamie and me, they made us sit together with our backs to the side of the boat in full view of them. One navigated, and the other guarded us with pistol ready at all times.

Another two hours and I saw the shoreline again. I nudged Jamie. "I got you back."

She smiled then said, "With a little help."

"That, my friend, is the story of my life. With a little help from my friends," and I sang those last seven words. The ratings ignored us. They had spotted the Okaloosa County Sheriff's Office Marine Unit boat approaching.

The Marine Unit boat was crewed by three Deputy Sheriffs, all veterans of law enforcement. They came alongside the *Aurora* to get a first-hand report from the coastguard ratings. On learning there was one dead body aboard, and two people in handcuffs, the senior Deputy, Nolan Peters rattled out his instructions. "Take the *Aurora* into the marina. By the time you are docked, the coroner should be there too. He'll make arrangements for the dead body to be taken to the morgue. As for the two suspects..."

I interrupted at that point. "Suspects? What the hell are you talking about? No one has asked us what happened."

"Sir, we will be asking some questions, rest assured of that," Peters said in his best sombre tone.

"Are we under arrest, or not?" I demanded. I know it was a bit rash of me, but I was getting pissed.

"No, I guess not," the officer said.

"Well then, will someone please let us out of these handcuffs?"

"Sir, once we have you safely aboard, we will attend to that."

He then looked past me and continued addressing the ratings, making a subtle point while he was at it. "Now…." hesitating for dramatic effect, "where was I?"

I decided to shut up and let things happen. Peters arranged for what he called 'evidence' to be handed over to one of his colleagues. One of the ratings gathered up Solley's pistol and the speargun. Handing them over to the deputies, he said without a trace of humour, "The spear stays with the dead body."

I swear if it weren't such a serious situation, I would have laughed. Jamie and I were then helped in stepping aboard the Marine Unit boat where we were both subjected to a pat-down search before Peters was satisfied he could order the handcuffs to be removed. "Any belongings on the *Aurora*?" he said.

"My purse. It's in the wheelhouse, and a blue cooler should be in there too," Jamie said.

"You will find my gun and windbreaker in her bag. I also have a red cooler and blue tee-shirt. They should be next to where you find Jamie's stuff," I said.

Calling over to the ratings, Peters said, "Did you hear that?" Once he heard an aye-aye, he added, "Bring them over here."

While we waited, Jamie and I rubbed our wrists to get the blood flowing once more. Once our belongings plus the 'evidence' had been stowed away, the Marine Unit cast away, heading for its base at Destin Harbor, followed by the *Aurora* with one dead body and a Coastguard inflatable towed in its wake.

CHAPTER FORTY-NINE

THE DETECTIVES

Peters spoke to me again shortly after getting underway. "I know you. You own Big Deals Gym in Destin."

"I do, and Jamie here is in charge of the martial arts instruction."

Jamie smiled, but Peters only acknowledged her with a curt, "Hello, ma'am." He turned to me again, saying, "You must be Matt Deal, then."

"I am, yes. Can I ask what's going to happen when we reach the shore?"

"We'll likely hand you both over to the Criminal Investigation Bureau. They will no doubt take your statements. Check it out, and if all is well, you will be released."

That was just what did happen. Detectives Antoniewicz and Myer first gave us our Miranda rights, then informed us we were arrested on suspicion of homicide: namely the slaying of Christine Solley. Jamie and I declined the presence of a lawyer, but before they interviewed us separately, they took my deck shoes and my shorts. They were now bagged up in evidence bags. As Myer handed me a white forensic suit to preserve my modesty, I noticed for the first time there were specks of what seemed like dried blood on both my shoes and shorts. I think that was what swung the decision to arrest us. While this procedure was happening, Jamie was led off by a female Deputy Sheriff to what I assumed was an interview room to await the detectives starting her interrogation. I couldn't help wondering if Jamie would be strip-searched and if so, would that cause her any embarrassment.

Once Jamie had gone, the two detectives took me to an interview room. As we walked down the corridor I looked through the narrow glass window of Interview Room 1. I saw Jamie sitting alone, drinking from what appeared to be a plastic cup. She seemed okay to me. I was shown into Interview Room 2, opposite from where I had seen Jamie.

What followed wasn't any kind of grilling. I simply told the detectives what had happened, and my statement was recorded on the machine in the room. It was such a full account they did not need to ask any questions. I'd covered all bases. About one hour later, they led me back to the processing area, where I was told to be seated and wait. Roughly after a further hour, Jamie was also shown through to the processing room. Detective Myer said, "That's it for now. I advise both of you not to leave Destin until this investigation is concluded."

That made me feel like I was in a Western movie, but I resisted the urge to smile. I simply said, "We won't. You know where to find us if you need anything."

Jamie and I were released at ten when our belongings were returned except my Glock and our cell phones. The detectives said they needed to check phone records for any contact between Solley and us. Well, there was. I told them all that in the interview. As for my gun, they wanted to check it out at ballistics to see if it had been fired recently. That made me want to laugh, but I resisted the urge to say it was a speargun, not a bullet that killed the crazy cop. I'm glad I did when I realised it wouldn't be until after the autopsy they would know for sure how Solley died.

A friendly Marine Unit cop gave us a ride to where I had left my car early that same morning. I wasn't concerned about the time because Anna knew it would be a long day, so it was no surprise to her that she had heard nothing from either Jamie or me. I had travelled light that day, meaning I had given my cell phone, gun and my windbreaker to Jamie to keep in her bag. It was quite a large bag too. Despite my time in the states, I could never get used to a bag of that size being called a purse. The cop and I joked about that before the cop dropped us at my car when I asked to use his cell phone, and he was kind enough to let me use it. I called Anna. "Hey, it's us. Be back soon. Any cold beers in the refrigerator?"

"Yes, catch anything?"

"Tell you the full story when I get home, baby. Is it okay if Jamie comes up to the deck with me?"

"Sure. Sounds like you two had a great time. See you soon."

"Okay, Jamie, let's go tell Anna the whole story," I said.

"You need me there?"

"Only if you want. I'm going to let Anna know you saved my life. I think you should be there."

"Okay," Jamie said.

The cop just nodded when I returned his phone, and as he dropped us at my car, he said, "Good luck, not that I think you'll need it."

CHAPTER FIFTY

NEWS TRAVELS FAST

I made my way to our home at Navarre Beach eager to see Anna and fill her in on such an unforgettable day. Pulling off the coastal highway, I parked the car on the cement driveway just short of the wooden piles driven deep into the ground that acted as stilts and supporting structure for the two-storey clapboard house. The deck lights were still on.

"Follow me, Jamie," I said realising she hadn't been to our home before. She grabbed her sweatshirt from her purse and put it on, no doubt owing to a slight chill in the breeze blowing off the ocean just a couple of hundred yards away.

Just before we were about to climb the wooden stairs, a car pulled up in the driveway right behind my Trailblazer. It was a car I didn't recognise, but I did recognise the voice as she called me through her open driver's window, "Matt, Sorry it's late, but I need a word… in private, please."

"Jamie, wait a moment please."

I walked over to the car, and through the open window, I looked at Mary Smyth, who said, "Matt, you need to see me first thing tomorrow. It's urgent."

"Can't you tell me now if it's that urgent," I said.

I heard the prolonged intake of breath before she said, "You will have to pull out of the election. Withdraw your candidacy."

"News travels fast. Is this because of Solley being killed?"

"Yes, and until the investigation is over and you're in the clear, applying for a clerking job is a futile exercise, never mind Sheriff of Walton County. Sorry, Matt, you have no choice."

"I understand," I said and did mean it, but I felt like crap.

As Mary Smyth started to back out her car onto the deserted coastal highway, she slid her door window down again and said, "I nearly forgot. Does the name Roly Fenney mean anything to you?"

"Yes," I said without explanation. "Why?"

"My son had a call from him a while back. He thought it was a bit weird because when my son confirmed you were running for sheriff, this Fenney just hung up."

"How does your son know Fenney?"

"They met at some climate change rally."

"Okay, thanks," I said.

I turned back to Jamie and said, "Let's go," as I watched my visitor back out safely and drive away.

On reaching the top of the stairs, I saw Anna coming out of the front door carrying some beers. On seeing us and undoubtedly my white forensic suit, she said, "What the hell have you been up to? And who was the visitor?"

"I'll change. Jamie can start to tell you what happened. I'll be out on the deck in a few moments, and I can also tell you all about our late-night visitor."

It was only a few moments as I hastily threw on some clean jogging pants and one of my favourite sweats. Making my way to the sliding patio door, I made my entrance to the deck patio area where Jamie was in the middle of recounting the essential parts of the day's events to Anna. As I took a seat at the patio table, Anna popped the ring on a can of cold beer and handed it to me together with a foam rubber holder, the sort Australians call stubby holders. Jamie had a beer can in her hand, also clad in foam rubber while Anna was drinking straight up mineral water.

Realising I was in the middle of Jamie's account, I said, "Carry on with the rest of the story."

Jamie did just that, and it was one-hundred percent complete and accurate as I listened to every word, watching the twinkling lights in the distant shipping lanes of the Gulf, feeling good to be alive in no small measure to friends like Jamie. From time to time, my gaze switched from the distant horizon to Anna's face across the table. I had never seen her looking so beautiful. Facing death does enhance all your senses.

On finishing her story, Jamie said, "I'm starving. I'll go make a sandwich if that's okay with you, Anna."

"Sure. There's not much in the refrigerator, but I have some corned beef and pickles in there. Open a fresh loaf too. And Jamie… thank you for what you did today. I will be forever grateful."

Jamie smiled, raised herself from her seat, and walking over to Anna kissed her on the cheek, saying softly, "Hey, sister. No problem. Anyways, we've all been to too many funerals lately."

Anna fought back a tear and replied, "Go! Make that sandwich and make mine pickles only. That's my food craving of the day. Makes a change from sushi."

We laughed before I added, "Throw some cheese on my corned beef and pickles."

"You got it!" Jamie said.

Anna waited a few moments before speaking once more. "Who was the visitor, then?"

"Mary Smyth," I said.

"What did she want?"

"Said it was best if I stand down from the election owing to what happened today."

"I must say, I'm relieved. It's all an omen if you ask me."

"No argument from me," I white-lied because I was disappointed. Changing tack, I said, "Hey, I had a premonition of sorts about Mickey Fretwell when I was out on the ocean today."

"I had more than a premonition, he called here about six hours ago," Anna said.

"Kidding, right? How would he know this number?"

"He called the gym. Sandy called me so when I knew who it was, I told her to ask him the name of your daughter and that of your ex. He answered both correctly then said, 'tell him flying stunt.' He will know what that means.'"

"Good work. Yes, it must be Mickey. The flying stunt refers to a narrow escape we had fleeing some armed bandits back in the UK. Did he call?"

"He did. He's here in the States and wants to visit."

"When?"

"He said in about six weeks. He's waiting on some news then he'll arrange to come over."

"That's fantastic. It will be great to catch up with Detective Mickey Fretwell."

Just then Jamie came back onto the deck carrying a tray, set with a plate of sandwiches, two beers and a bowl filled with potato chips. "You need more water, Anna?" she inquired before sitting.

"I'm fine," Anna said, shaking her head. "Which are the pickles only?"

"The ones with the cocktail sticks in them. I made it like a club sandwich for you," Jamie said.

"Thanks. Matt has some more news for you," Anna said.

I went on to fill in Jamie with the history of Detective Mickey Fretwell and our escapades while working Robbery-Homicide together on the UK's National Crime Agency. I left nothing out, including the facts behind how and why I killed Tommy Etchwell and how that led to me coming back to Destin. Jamie sat eating her sandwich and taking the odd glug from her beer, but I could tell she was captivated by my deeds and misdeeds back in England.

When I had finished, she said, "Robbery-Homicide? I thought that was an American law enforcement term."

I explained, "It is. After the UK went to the dogs when it left Europe and crime rates rocketed, the government formed the NCA. It's modelled on the L.A.P.D."

"I see. And Elaine Steele worked there too?"

"Yes, she was my partner before Fretwell. I can tell you, he took a lot of getting used to. He got on my nerves all the time, but something changed all that."

"Intriguing? What was that?" Jamie said.

"He took a bullet for me."

"We will have to form a club and make a tee shirt. 'WE TOOK A BULLET FOR MATT DEAL.' Jamie laughed.

"Technically, you didn't, but I take your point. Without you and Mickey Fretwell intervening I wouldn't be here now," I said. "Talking about saving my life, where did you learn how to use a speargun?"

"Scuba diving when I lived in Corpus Christi. I used to do it often and became a bit of an expert with spearguns," Jamie said.

"I'm so glad you did," I said.

"Okay, enough talk about all that stuff. Mister and miss, I need my beauty sleep so finish your beer and sandwich and let's call it a night. Jamie, you can sleep in the spare room tonight. Matt Deal, come to bed soon." Anna smiled at Jamie as she issued her commands. "Jamie, before I forget, have you called Pat to tell him about today?"

"No. The police kept our cell phones. I'll call early in the morning from here if you don't mind."

"No problem. Use my cell phone or the landline. Call now if you like," Anna said, handing Jamie her cell phone with Pat's number still on speed dial.

Jamie took the phone and let it ring out for a while before giving up. "No answer," she said.

CHAPTER FIFTY-ONE

FREEDOM TRUCKING

One Week Later

Anna and I were reading at home when I heard a truck pull up outside. Not a regular pickup truck, the noise was louder and more like a tractor unit. I immediately thought of Pat, but why would he turn up unannounced in the rig he'd just purchased in New Orleans.

Opening the front door, I walked across to the guard rail so I could see down to the driveway. Even in the light from the adjacent streetlamps, I could make out it was a black rig, and I could also see the new decals on the driver's door proudly stating this was a truck operated by Freedom Trucking of

Destin, Florida, the name of Pat's new venture. I switched on the outside lighting so I could safely make my way down the external stairs to the driveway.

As I stepped onto the cement, Pat was climbing down from the tractor unit. Before he closed the driver's door, I swear I saw him push a large dog back into the cab. He jumped down from the last step onto the driveway and looked startled on seeing me standing there. "Matt," Pat stuttered.

"Pat, what's up, my friend? And did I see a dog in there?"

"Jamie and I wanted to surprise you."

"What, by driving up in a great big black rig that must weigh all of ten-thousand pounds?"

"Twenty-thousand," Pat corrected me. "Does Anna know I'm here?"

"Not yet, why?"

"Look." Pat opened the driver's door once more and was forced to stop the dog from jumping the considerable distance from the cab to the driveway. He put a leash on the dog's collar and guided it slowly down to the ground with a few grunts as the dog was huge and undoubtedly heavy.

"What the hell," I said. "He's nearly a double for Sheba. Is the eye patch real or for show?"

"Real. The dog's she, not he…" Pat paused when he saw me chuckle. "What's funny?" he asked.

"Nothing, Pat. Really… nothing."

I wasn't sure Pat was convinced as he looked puzzled, but he continued, "Found her in a dog pound in New Orleans. She got shot in the eye with a BB gun and lost sight in that eye. Can you believe it was her owner who shot her? Bastard!"

"His loss, Anna's gain. I assume it's a gift for Anna."

"Better had been," Anna said as quietly as she had made her approach. "Sheba, come here, girl," she said.

The dog may have started life with another name, but now this one-eyed German Shepherd with an eyepatch was Anna's Sheba - owner and dog with matching eyepatches. As she was fussing the dog, I noticed she had thrown her leather jacket over her shoulders to keep out the evening chill—the one I hadn't seen for some time. My mind raced back to the night I had met her at Destin Beach – the night Mercy was attacked. I recalled seeing that same jacket with a patch on the back – *A wolf, or maybe a German Shepherd with an eye patch over the canine's right eye,* were my exact thoughts at that time. Now, I knew it was a German Shepherd.

CHAPTER FIFTY-TWO

THE NEW SHERIFF

Six weeks after the adoption of Sheba

"You are kidding me!" I said it so loud all the folks in the restaurant looked at our table to see what had caused the commotion.

They didn't hear what Mickey Fretwell just said to cause my outburst of delight and surprise. "I'm the new Sheriff of Walton County. It's not official yet, but I got a call from Mary Smyth this morning telling me the count is in and there'll be an official announcement tomorrow."

Fretwell had called me the day previously to arrange a meetup. I suggested he come to the gym so I could introduce him to everybody, then take lunch in the restaurant a couple of doors away from the gym. He readily agreed after he had extended his condolences about Mercy's passing and almost in the same breath offered his congratulations to Anna and me on the forthcoming marriage and birth of our child. I thanked him of course, but saved all else for when we met face to face.

Now over lunch with Anna, Jamie and Sandy, we chatted over old times in England and caught up on events since I had returned to Florida. "How long have you been in the States?" I said.

"Three months now. Under the new visa scheme, I got cleared for detective grade in Baltimore because of my service with the NCA and the UK has special immigration status now it's virtually another state in the Union. That also qualifies me for fast track citizenship, again under the new rules that favour the UK, but only to citizens with a solid record in professions like law enforcement. That's how I was able to qualify for the office of Sheriff in Walton County. Technically, I will be Sheriff-Elect for six months until my citizenship is ratified, thanks to Mary Smyth bending the rules a bit."

"That all makes sense, because this country needs qualified law enforcement people more than ever with the high rates of homicide and racial divide, not to mention the proliferation of extreme right-wing factions," I said, giving him an inkling as to the current political situation in the U.S. of A.

"You are talking about the Neo-Nazis?" Fretwell said.

"Them, and all the groups that are just anti-everything. It's a problem that's existed for decades but has got worse over time."

"So, worse than back in the UK?"

"I would say so, yes. Anyway, back to you. What about your gunshot wound? I suppose they gave you a medical."

"Fully recovered, Matt. I was a while in a wheelchair after Etchwell shot me but resumed active duties before I took over Emily Breen's old position."

"You? Head of NCA Internal Affairs?"

"Yes. That's one of the reasons Mary Smyth encouraged me to run for Sheriff. She's keen on clearing out the nests of corruption on the law enforcement side. I understand you know something about that."

"Sure do, buddy, and if you need my help, just call, okay?"

"I'm calling right now. How does Chief of Detectives sound?"

"Me? Walton County? Sounds fine, but you need to know something."

"Deputy Sheriff Christine Solley, by any chance? Forget it. You will be receiving a letter soon… both of you," Fretwell looked over to Jamie, "exonerating you both of any culpability. It will be recorded as justifiable homicide, and I know the inquest will record the same verdict for sure."

"She was part of this nest of corruption as you so adroitly put it."

"So I understand. Matt, tell me this. If we ever get to the bottom of the missing DNA and possibly even retrieve it, what's your attitude to re-opening the case against those responsible?"

I paused to think.

"Mickey, I'm not sure is my honest answer. I have mixed emotions about it. On the one hand, what's done is done. What would it achieve by dragging it into court apart from bad memories? On the other…"

I didn't know for sure what I was about to add and maybe just as well because Micky Fretwell interrupted. "Okay, I understand that. I just needed to take a rain check, okay?"

"No problem. I'm glad you asked. Is your offer still on the table?"

"Of course. Some ground rules, though. You call me Sheriff and I call you Chief," Fretwell said.

"On one condition," I said.

"Yes?"

"The Sheriff makes sure my cell phone and gun are returned to me by Destin Marine Unit."

"Not my jurisdiction, is it?" Fretwell said seriously.

"I can see you need a geography lesson, Mickey," and we both laughed, partly at how far we had both come since our detective days in England.

CHAPTER FIFTY-THREE

THUGS

The reunion was interrupted by the loud noise of motorcycle engines revving right outside on the highway. We all turned to look. There were possibly as many as forty bikes outside. That wasn't the problem. Each machine was ridden by the scariest looking thugs Destin had seen in a long time. They didn't look like the average Hells Angel. They appeared to be a Neo-Nazi outfit replete with large swastika patches on the back of their leathers. Some wore replica *stahlhelm*, steel Nazi Germany style helmets. The rest wore nothing on their heads save for a bandana with a clenched fist symbol and most sported long straggly beards.

"You get much of that?" Fretwell said in his casual, understated British manner.

"No. Never seen anything like that before. Weird, as they were Georgia plates on those bikes," I replied.

"There's something else you need to know, Matt. Some bad news from the UK."

"Okay, tell me."

"Perry Etchwell is in the States."

"I don't know a Perry Etchwell."

"He's the son of Terry Etchwell, and he's sworn that he's going to track you down and kill you for what you did to his father," Fretwell said.

"Thanks for the warning. Are you sure you want to be closely associated with me?"

"Can't think of anyone better. That's why I want you as my chief of detectives."

"Thanks, I do appreciate it," I said. "And did I ever tell you I appreciated the way you acted that day I killed Tommy Etchwell? If it hadn't been for you shooting some of his goons, I would never have got the opportunity to kill Etchwell."

"You didn't because you skipped the country."

I stood and walked around the table. Fretwell also got up from his chair, and as he did so I gave him a warm man hug. "Thank you," was all I said.

I motioned to Anna to come to sit closer to us, now Fretwell and I had finished our bonding and catching up on the old times. "Happy to see you are still good friends. It's like a Brit invasion, not that I'm complaining," she said.

"I guess you are used to our British accents, then," Mickey Fretwell said.

"What was that you said?" Anna said, then laughed. "Yes. I'm used to it now."

"So, if I may ask. What's the wedding plans? Set a date yet?" Fretwell asked.

"We will wait until our baby is born. So, sometime after August. Matt and I agreed we wanted her there at the wedding. We want her to be part of the wedding pictures. Funny, I know, but that's what we want."

"Nice."

CHAPTER FIFTY-FOUR

THREATS

Eight Weeks Later

Sandy Grant called me at home, urging me to come to the gym office. She made it clear it was something that I needed to see urgently. Anna and I had just finished breakfast, so I wasted no time and drove for forty minutes before I parked the Trailblazer outside the gym.

Sandy buzzed me in as it was quicker than keying in the code to access the office upstairs. As I entered the office, Sandy was sitting behind her manager's desk and handed me a printout straightaway. "You need to read this," she said.

It was clear it was a printout of an email addressed to sales@bigdealsgym.com, one of the gym's generic email addresses. I quickly glanced at the sending address. It didn't make sense to me as it was a jumble of alphanumeric symbols.

The body of the email read:

DEAL. THE SHOW OF FORCE AT YOUR GYM RECENTLY WAS A WARNING.

MERCY IS DEAD. STAY OUT OF OLD SCORES. IF YOU DON'T YOU AND YOUR FAMILY WILL JOIN MERCY.

Unsurprisingly, there was no name to help identify the sender. "Sandy, is this the only copy?" I said.

"Yes, Matt. Do you want more?"

"No. Here, take this one and keep it locked away in the office," I said, handing Sandy the printout. "And don't mention this to anyone unless I tell you differently."

"You got it."

My detective head got into gear. *This is about Mercy. Is there a connection between Solley and the rapists? If so, what is it? What has a group of biker outlaws got to do with it all?* I knew I had to wait a while longer for

Fretwell to appoint me as his chief of detectives, but this couldn't be delayed. My family was at risk.

Leaving the office and driving to nearby Miramar Beach where Fretwell had rented a condo, I made two phone calls. The first to Anna and without purposely alarming her, to make sure she had her Glock close at all times and ensured all doors were locked. Typically for Anna, she calmly said, "No problem. Sheba will let me know if we have visitors, wanted or not. I take it these are precautions, otherwise you'd be here." Sheba was now kept in a dog cage in the empty space under the house, one big enough to allow her plenty of movement. She had turned out to be an excellent guard dog, barking at any visitor who pulled up in our driveway.

"I'm not sure what I'm dealing with, right now. I'll talk to you later after I see Mickey Fretwell."

"Okay, Matt. Give him my regards."

Thirty minutes later, I had found the Miramar Beach condo overlooking the Gulf. Mickey buzzed me in through the security doors once I had spoken with him on the intercom system. Settling into a vast new sofa he had just bought, I got straight to the subject. "Mickey. Remember you asked me about my thoughts on re-opening the case against the rapists?"

"I do. What you got in mind?"

"I'm all for it, and I'll tell you why."

After I recounted the story of receiving the threatening email, Fretwell said, "You think that's connected to Mercy's rape?"

"I do. What else can it be?"

"I'm not sure, Matt. All you have at the moment is a hunch."

"Mickey, that's what good detectives are about. Hunches, gut instinct built upon years of experience."

"I take your point. What do you want me to do?"

"Speed up my appointment, for one, so I can take over the investigation."

"That is not going to happen, Matt. It would be a conflict of interest."

"Okay, I see that, but you head it up with me riding shotgun. How does that sound?"

"I don't have a problem with that. My first day in the new job is next Monday. I'm on some kind of moving in leave right now. I will make sure your appointment is fast-tracked once I start. Is that okay?"

"Sounds good. In the meantime, can you find out if Solley's home was searched after she got killed?"

"It was, Matt. We didn't find anything, but her laptop and cell phone are still being examined by the tech team."

"Good. That's good because my instinct tells me Solley is more involved in all this than anyone knew."

"Leave it with me. Now, I'm ready for a coffee and I don't have any here. Want to join me? It's only a few doors down. There's a great coffee shop there."

"Lead the way," I said.

Fretwell was right. The 'At Home' coffee shop served up fabulous brewed coffee and Mickey enjoyed a blueberry muffin, seeing he had skipped breakfast. The shop was one of four in a small strip-mall at the end of the road. It was the end too, as the beach was just past the wire fencing marking the point where traffic was forced to turn about. It was deserted, as were the other stores and the small parking area in front of the mall. I declined any food but was enjoying my coffee, first calling Anna to check all was okay at home, before chatting to Fretwell. She told me she was fine and to stop worrying. I thought how stupid that sounded but didn't say it.

Finishing the call to Anna, I was just about to carry on talking to Fretwell when I saw a Harley ride by. I knew it had to turn around and I instinctively drew my Glock from my holster, not because it was a motorcycle but rather the look of the rider. He was dressed in the same way as those who had caused the uproar outside my gym. Then, it clicked with me I was looking at a Georgia plate at the back of the bike as it first rode by. Now, and not by instinct but as a deliberate act, I checked my Glock. I unclipped the magazine, and all was good. Clipping it back, I chambered a round and placed my gun under the table, resting it on my right thigh, so it was out of sight.

"Mickey, any moment now the door will open. Whatever else you do, do not turn to look, okay?" Before he could answer, I called the young lady, the only server in the coffee shop. "Miss! Go into the storage room. Now! Please don't ask any questions."

She disappeared from view as the coffee shop door opened. The biker, with a bandana covering the lower part of his face, was carrying a pump-action shotgun. He took two steps inside the small shop before he started to raise the gun. That was what I was waiting for. Without standing, I pulled the Glock from its resting place and fired. One, two, three, four times, in rapid succession. Four body shots struck the biker in his torso. He dropped to the floor instantly.

Rushing over to the biker, I could see he was still breathing. Kneeling next to his face, I said, "Who sent you? Who is paying you?"

The man tried to say something, but it was masked by a gurgling noise accompanied by a red froth spilling from his open mouth. He somehow cleared his throat and uttered his dying words. "Don't matter, Deal. Someone else will come before you are made Sheriff." His eyes rolled back, and his head fell to one side. It was only then I became aware of Fretwell standing there with the shotgun in his hand.

"I got the shotgun for evidence. What was that about you and Sheriff?"

"That, my friend, proves Solley is the key to all this. It was only after Jamie killed her that certain folks knew I had pulled out from the election. She must have set something in train but that something, and those killers, still think I'm going to be sheriff. They don't know you are the new sheriff."

"Right, I follow that, and it's clear they don't want any more digging into Mercy's case and the missing DNA evidence."

"You got it, so the quicker you get me that chief's shield, the better. And one more thing, Mickey," I said.

"What?"

"Where's your weapon?"

"Didn't think I'd need it. It's back in the condo."

"Never think, Sheriff. Carry it at all times and be ready to use it. Welcome to America."

THE END

AFTERWORD

I would like to take this opportunity to apologise to the respective police departments of Walton County Sheriff's Office and the Okaloosa County Sheriff's Office both of which are in Florida's Panhandle.

I'm a believer in using real places in my fiction writing because as the publisher's disclaimer states at the front of the book: *Locales and public names are sometimes used for atmospheric purposes.*

However, in *Mercy*, Book One in the Detective Matt Deal Thrillers, I erroneously placed Destin in the wrong jurisdiction. I now know it is within the jurisdiction of Okaloosa County Sheriff's Office. For that mistake, I am sorry. I should have known better as I used to be a frequent visitor to the area. So, I hope the readers and both sheriff's offices will forgive me for that *faux pas*, especially those readers who know the area far better than I.

It should go without saying that any references to corruption or any other malpractices within either of those law enforcement departments are purely elements of my imagination and fiction writing and are used only for dramatic effect.

ABOUT THE AUTHOR

Stephen Bentley is a former UK police Detective Sergeant, pioneering undercover cop, and barrister (criminal trial attorney). He is now a freelance writer and an occasional contributor to Huffington Post UK on undercover policing, and mental health issues.

His bestselling memoir, 'Undercover: Operation Julie - The Inside Story,' is a frank and fascinating insight into his undercover detective experiences during Operation Julie - an elite group of detectives who successfully investigated one of the world's largest drug rings. It has now been adapted for a feature film.

Stephen also writes crime fiction in a fast-paced plot-driven style including the Steve Regan Undercover Cop Thriller and the Detective Matt Deal Thriller series.

One of his short stories, 'The Rose Slayer,' won the SIA murder mystery competition in 2018, and has now been published in a multi-author anthology of murder mystery short stories, titled 'Death Among Us.'

His fiction draws heavily on his law enforcement background adding that ingredient of authenticity about which the legendary Raymond Chandler opined, "Fiction in any form has always intended to be realistic," when writing about "the detective story" in his essay 'The Simple Art of Murder'(1950). Stephen subscribes to that school of thought.

When he isn't writing, Stephen relaxes on the beaches of the Philippines with his family where he now lives, often with a cold beer and a book to hand.

You may find him on Twitter as @StephenBentley8 or connect with him at https://www.stephenbentley.info/ where you may subscribe to his mailing list by downloading your free eBook – *The Secret: A Prequel to the Steve Regan Undercover Cop Thrillers.*

ALSO BY STEPHEN BENTLEY

NON-FICTION

Undercover: Operation Julie – The Inside Story

How to Drive Like an Idiot in Bacolod

FICTION

Standalone

Comfort Zone: A Tale of Suspense

Death Among Us: An Anthology of Murder Mystery Short Stories (multi-authors)

The Detective Matt Deal Thrillers

Mercy

Mayhem

The Steve Regan Undercover Cop Thriller Series

The Secret

*Who The F*ck Am I?*

Dilemma

Rivers of Blood